双 语 名 著 无 障 碍 阅 读 丛 书

第四级

欧·亨利短篇小说精选

The Essential O.Henry Collection

[美国] 欧·亨利 著

张经浩 译

中国出版集团

中译出版社

图书在版编目（CIP）数据

欧·亨利短篇小说精选：英汉对照/（美）欧·亨利（Henry, O.）著；张经浩译. —北京：中译出版社，2012.7（2017.4重印）
（双语名著无障碍阅读丛书）
ISBN 978-7-5001-3464-0

I. ①欧… II. ①欧… ②张… III. ①英语—汉语—对照读物
②短篇小说—小说集—美国—近代 IV. ①H319.4：I

中国版本图书馆CIP数据核字（2012）第149806号

出版发行 / 中译出版社
地　　址 / 北京市西城区车公庄大街甲4号物华大厦六层
电　　话 /（010）68359827；　68359303（发行部）；　53601537（编辑部）
邮　　编 / 100044
传　　真 /（010）68357870
电子邮箱 / book@ctph.com.cn
网　　址 / http://www.ctph.com.cn

出版策划 / 张高里
策划编辑 / 胡晓凯
责任编辑 / 胡晓凯　范祥镇
封面设计 / 潘　峰

排　　版 / 陈　彬
印　　刷 / 保定市中画美凯印刷有限公司
经　　销 / 新华书店

规　　格 / 710毫米×1000毫米　1/16
印　　张 / 13
字　　数 / 160千
版　　次 / 2012年7月第一版
印　　次 / 2017年4月第五次

ISBN 978-7-5001-3464-0　　　　　　定价：18.00元

　　多年以来，中译出版社有限公司（原中国对外翻译出版有限公司）凭借国内一流的翻译和出版实力及资源，精心策划、出版了大批双语读物，在海内外读者中和业界内产生了良好、深远的影响，形成了自己鲜明的出版特色。

　　二十世纪八九十年代出版的英汉（汉英）对照"一百丛书"，声名远扬，成为一套最权威、最有特色且又实用的双语读物，影响了一代又一代英语学习者和中华传统文化研究者、爱好者；还有"英若诚名剧译丛""中华传统文化精粹丛书""美丽英文书系"，这些优秀的双语读物，有的畅销，有的常销不衰反复再版，有的被选为大学英语阅读教材，受到广大读者的喜爱，获得了良好的社会效益和经济效益。

　　"双语名著无障碍阅读丛书"是中译专门为中学生和英语学习者精心打造的又一品牌，是一个新的双语读物系列，具有以下特点：

　　选题创新——该系列图书是国内第一套为中小学生量身打造的双语名著读物，所选篇目均为教育部颁布的语文新课标必读书目，或为中学生以及同等文化水平的社会读者喜闻乐见的世界名著，重新编译为英汉（汉英）对照的双语读本。这些书既给青少年读者提供了成长过程中不可或缺的精神食粮，又让他们领略到原著的精髓和魅力，对他们更好地学习英文大有裨益；同时，丛书中入选的《论语》《茶馆》《家》等汉英对照读物，亦是热爱中国传统文化的中外读者所共知的经典名篇，能使读者充分享受阅读经典的无限乐趣。

无障碍阅读——中学生阅读世界文学名著的原著会遇到很多生词和文化难点。针对这一情况，我们给每一本读物原文中的较难词汇和不易理解之处都加上了注释，在内文的版式设计上也采取英汉（或汉英）对照方式，扫清了学生阅读时的障碍。

优良品质——中译双语读物多年来在读者中享有良好口碑，这得益于作者和出版者对于图书质量的不懈追求。"双语名著无障碍阅读丛书"继承了中译双语读物的优良传统——精选的篇目、优秀的译文、方便实用的注解，秉承着对每一个读者负责的精神，竭力打造精品图书。

愿这套丛书成为广大读者的良师益友，愿读者在英语学习和传统文化学习两方面都取得新的突破。

法国最杰出的短篇小说家要数莫泊桑，俄国的当推契诃夫，美国独树一帜的则是欧·亨利。

欧·亨利（O. Henry）真名威廉·西德尼·波特（William Sydney Porter）。据说，"欧·亨利"是法国药剂大师艾蒂安·欧西安·亨利（Etienne-Ossian Henry）的名字的节略。

1862年9月11日，欧·亨利生于美国北卡罗来纳州格林斯伯格的一个医生家。三岁丧母，幼时在堂亲办的一所私立学校读书，十五岁开始在本地一家药房当学徒。十九岁那年，格林斯伯格一位医生见他身体不好，带他到西部得克萨斯州拉萨尔县一个牧场做客，欧·亨利很喜爱西部牧场的生活，在那儿竟住了两年。

1885年，欧·亨利认识了一位十七岁的姑娘阿索尔·埃斯蒂斯（Athol Estes）。1887年7月5日夜，姑娘刚念完中学，便瞒着父母与欧·亨利双双跑到牧师家。在美国，婚姻经牧师认可便算合法。姑娘的母亲本希望女儿嫁个有钱人，得知情况后气得不可开交。

但两人琴瑟调和。新婚妻子鼓动丈夫写作，而欧·亨利果然当年就在《底特律自由报刊与真实》上发表了作品。次年阿索尔生一子，可惜襁褓中便夭亡。第二年又生一女，取名玛格丽特（Margaret）。

1891年，欧·亨利到奥斯汀的第一国民银行当出纳员。到1894年，欧·亨利花250元买下奥斯汀的一家周刊，更名《滚石》，他既当编辑又当出版商，自写文章自作画。英语中有句谚语，叫"滚石不长苔"，但欧·亨利却发现他的《滚石》滚了一年后眼见长了苔，于是作罢，让这家周刊又回归了原主。

也就是在1894年10月，联邦银行检查员发现欧·亨利的账目有问题，欧·亨利只好辞职。1896年2月，欧·亨利受到盗用公款的起诉，被传受审。本来他的案情并不严重，但他逃到了新奥尔良，后又流浪到中美洲的洪都拉斯。1897年，他获悉身患结核的妻子病危，才赶回奥斯汀。后即被捕，但又被保释出狱。出狱不久，妻子病故。第二年，被判有罪，处五年徒刑，在俄亥俄州首府哥伦市的联邦监狱服刑。

欧·亨利因一技之长当了监狱的药剂师。也就是在服刑期间，他开始认真写作，以"欧·亨利"为笔名发表小说。服刑三年零三个月后，欧·亨利提前获释。

1902年欧·亨利移居纽约，成了专业作家。这年，他正好四十岁整。尽管他没有忘记早年的快乐，却看到了生活的阴暗面。在纽约，由于大量佳作出版，他名利双收。他不仅挥霍无度，而且赌博，好酒贪杯。写作的劳累与生活的无节制使他的身体受到严重损伤。1907年，欧·亨利再婚。可惜，第二次婚姻对他来说并没有什么幸福可言。1910年6月3日，他病倒了。两天后，即6月5日，他与世长辞，死于肝硬化，年仅48岁。

欧·亨利的小说最显著、最为人熟知和称道的特点是结尾出人意料。作家在故事情节发展过程中，将某一方面着力描写。当然，这些描写与主题是密切相关的，但并没有触及最重要的事实，最重要的事实只用一两笔带过，连最细心的读者也难以看出作家埋下的伏笔。到故事收尾时，笔锋一转，写出了一个完全意想不到的结局。这时，读者再一回想整个情节，会为作家构思的巧妙拍案叫绝。

欧·亨利的写作不以任何作家为楷模。他常读法国小说家莫泊桑的作品，但并没有以莫泊桑为师。他创作时并不考虑什么创作的规矩，怎样想来就怎样写。然而，他的写作始终有一个明确的目的：供读者消遣。也许由于这个原因，还没有哪位评论家说过欧·亨利曾深受某某人的影响，他的小说才有意料之外情理之中的结局，才受到广大读者喜爱。

尽管欧·亨利写小说时一心想给读者消遣，他的作品却远不全是喜剧和滑稽剧。他也写悲剧，而且数量不少。他最优秀的小说《圣贤的礼物》就是个悲剧。欧·亨利也写男女之情，但不像别的作家，是为歌颂爱情的永恒。他的这类小说总要出现读者意想不到的情况，令读者或者一笑，或者一叹，或者一惊。这些小说当然说明欧·亨利构思的巧妙，具有独创天才，但同时从中也可看出他为供读者消遣而写作的目的。

欧·亨利是位有独特风格的杰出短篇小说家，以巧妙的构思、夸张和幽默的文笔反映了他那个时代的人和事。他的作品与声誉早已越出了美国的国界。但要用另一国文字传达作家作品的风貌谈何容易！

笔者进行文学翻译历来一求正确理解原作之意，二求清楚传达原作之意，三求多多保存原作风味。笔者历来也反对"翻译腔"。外译汉时，译文应是流畅的汉语，汉译外时，译文应是流畅的外语。只有在原文不流畅时，译文才会不流畅，但这只是特例。

然而，翻译是一种艺术，翻译毕竟很难，而本人能力又有限，实际效果与主观愿望会存在一段距离。甚至，失误也在所难免。

欧·亨利是美国独树一帜的短篇小说一代大师，最杰出的作家之一。本集出版如能使读者领略这位大师的独特风采，译者的劳动便算是得到了最大报偿。"知我罪我，唯在读者"！

译者

目
CONTENTS
录

O. Henry

这是一个有关时光、有关友情的故事。

站在时光隧道这一端的人，可知道，滚滚而逝的时光足以改变我们的人生轨迹、相貌，甚至品质。现在的知己好友，二十年后，也许是南辕北辙的两个世界里的人。

我们会怀旧，往昔的美好使我们眷恋，过去的情感牵动着我们的追思。然而，当二十年过去，蓦然回首，物是人非，怎不让人唏嘘感叹！

After Twenty Years

The policeman **on the beat**[1] moved up the avenue **impressively**[2]. The impressiveness was habitual and not for show, for spectators were few. The time was barely 10 o'clock at night, but chilly gusts of wind with a taste of rain in them had well nigh depeopled the streets.

Trying doors as he went, **twirling**[3] his club with many **intricate**[4] and artful movements, turning now and then to cast his watchful eye adown the **pacific**[5] thoroughfare, the officer, with his **stalwart**[6] form and slight **swagger**[7], made a fine picture of a guardian of the peace. The **vicinity**[8] was one that kept early hours. Now and then you might see the lights of a cigar store or of an all-night lunch counter; but the majority of the doors belonged to business places that had long since been closed.

When about midway of a certain block the policeman suddenly slowed his walk. In the doorway of a darkened hardware store a man leaned, with an unlighted cigar in his mouth. As the policeman walked up to him the man spoke up quickly.

"It's all right, officer," he said, **reassuringly**[9], "I'm just waiting for a friend. It's an appointment made twenty years ago. Sounds a little funny to you, doesn't it? Well, I'll explain if you'd like to make

· 004 ·

二十年后

① on the beat 执行巡逻任务
② impressively /ɪmˈpresɪvlɪ/
ad. 威严地,使人敬畏地

of wind that is blowing]
[a sudden strong expression of
emotion]
③ twirl /twɜːl/ v. 使快速旋转
parts and small details that fit together]
④ intricate /ˈɪntrɪkɪt/ a. 复杂精细的
⑤ pacific /pəˈsɪfɪk/ a 宁静的,平静的
⑥ stalwart /ˈstɔːlwət/ a. 健壮的;结实的
part of a group of people or things
⑦ swagger /ˈswægə/ n. 昂首阔步
⑧ vicinity /vɪˈsɪnɪtɪ/ n. 附近地区

ing to prove that what they said is not true]

⑨ reassuringly
/ˌriːəˈʃʊərɪŋlɪ/ ad. 安慰地,鼓励地
connected with their work]

一位巡警在马路上威风凛凛地走着。他的威武是习惯成自然,而不是摆给人看的架势,因为行人已少而又少。时间还不到夜晚十点,但眼见要下雨,冷风一阵紧似一阵,马路上就已是空空荡荡了。

他边走边检查各家的房门,还不时转过头,用警惕的目光向平静的通衢大道两头远望,那甩警棍的动作多姿多彩,再加上体格魁伟,却不带傲气,看起来是好一个太平天下的卫士的形象。这一带收市早。你偶尔看到还亮着灯的店或者是烟店,或者是通宵餐馆,大多数店铺却早早关了门。

走到一个路段的正中时,警察突然放慢了脚步。一家灭了灯的五金店门口,有个男子斜靠门站着,嘴里叼了根烟,并没点着。看到警察走过来他抢先说话了。

"没事,警官,我在等一位朋友,"他镇定自若地说,"二十年前约好现在相见。你听了觉得奇怪,是吗?你要是不放心呢,我可以把事情说

certain it's all **straight**①. About that long ago there used to be a restaurant where this store stands — 'Big Joe' Brady's restaurant."

"Until five years ago," said the policeman. "It was torn down then."

The man in the doorway struck a match and lit his cigar. The light showed a pale, square-jawed face with keen eyes, and a little white scar near his right eyebrow. His **scarfpin**② was a large diamond, oddly set.

"Twenty years ago to-night," said the man, "I dined here at 'Big Joe' Brady's with Jimmy Wells, my best **chum**③, and the finest chap in the world. He and I were raised here in New York, just like two brothers, together. I was eighteen and Jimmy was twenty. The next morning I was to start for the West to **make my fortune**④. You couldn't have dragged Jimmy out of New York; he thought it was the only place on earth. Well, we agreed that night that we would meet here again exactly twenty years from that date and time, no matter what our conditions might be or from what distance we might have to come. We figured that in twenty years each of us ought to have our destiny worked out and our fortunes made, whatever they were going to be."

"It sounds pretty interesting," said the policeman. "Rather a long time between meets, though, it seems to me. Haven't you heard from your friend since you left?"

"Well, yes, for a time we **corresponded**⑤," said the other. "But after a year or two we **lost track of**⑥ each other. You see, the West is a pretty big proposition, and I kept **hustling**⑦ around over it pretty lively. But I know Jimmy will meet me here if he's alive, for he always was the truest, **stanchest**⑧ old chap in the world. He'll never forget. I came a thousand miles to stand in this door to-night, and it's worth it if my old partner **turns up**⑨."

给你听听。二十年前，这家店是一家餐馆，叫大乔·布雷迪餐馆。"

"餐馆早五年就没有了。"警察说。

站在店门边的人划着了根火柴点烟。火柴光一照，只见这人长着个方下巴，脸色发白，目光倒炯炯有神，右边眉毛附近留着个小白伤疤。领带扣针歪别着，上面镶着颗大钻石。

那人说："二十年前，我跟吉米·韦尔斯在这儿的餐馆吃饭。他是我最要好的哥儿们，世界上顶呱呱的小子。我俩是在纽约长大的，亲亲热热像兄弟俩。我十八岁，吉米二十岁。第二天我要去西部闯荡。在吉米看来天下似乎只有一个纽约。你就是拽也无法把他拽出纽约，那天晚上，我们约定，就从那一天那一刻算起，整整二十年后在这地方再会面，不论我们的处境如何，也不论要走多远的路。我想，过了这二十年，好歹各人也该知道了自己的命运，混出了点名堂。"

"这事倒挺新鲜。时隔二十年才又见上一面，未免太久了点。分手以后你知道你朋友的消息吗？"警察问。

那人答道："说起来我们也有过一段书信往来，但过了一两年便断了联系。你知道西部那边地方有多大，而我来来往往又行踪无定。但是我知道要是吉米还活着，准会上这儿来找我。要说忠诚可靠，这老兄天底下数第一，他绝不会忘。今天晚上我千里迢迢跑到这家店门口等着，如果老朋友当真来，跑这一趟值得。"

① straight /streɪt/ a. 规矩的 *dull and boring*

② scarfpin /ˈskɑːfpɪn/ n. 领带针 *protest is left on the skin after a wound has healed* *to happen very much*

③ chum /tʃʌm/ n. 好友

④ make one's fortune 发财，发迹

⑤ correspond /ˌkɒrɪˈspɒnd/ v. 通信 *or what will happen to them in the future, especially things that they cannot change or avoid* *less important sth. else*

⑥ lose track of 失去与……的联系

⑦ hustle /ˈhʌsl/ v. 奔忙 *in a rough aggressive way*

⑧ stanch /stɑːntʃ/ a. 坚固的，可靠的 *busy noisy activity of a lot of people in one place*

⑨ turn up 出现，露面

The waiting man pulled out a handsome watch, the lids of it set with small diamonds.

"Three minutes to ten," he announced. "It was exactly ten o'clock when we parted here at the restaurant door."

[~from sb) (formal) If a person parts from another person, or two people part, they leave each

"Did pretty well out West, didn't you?" asked the policeman.

"**You bet!** [1] I hope Jimmy has done half as well. He was a kind of [(informal) a way of referring to a man or boy]

plodder[2], though, good fellow as he was. I've had to compete with [a person who works slowly and steadily but without imagination]

some of the sharpest wits going to **get my pile**[3]. A man gets in a **groove**[4] [the ability to say or write things that are both clever and

in New York. It takes the West to put a razor-edge on him.

The policeman twirled his club and took a step or two.

"I'll be on my way. Hope your friend comes around all right. Going to call time on him sharp?"

"I should say not!" said the other. "I'll give him half an hour at least. If Jimmy is alive on earth he'll be here by that time. So long, officer." [the area which a police office walks around regularly and which he or

"Good-night, sir," said the policeman, passing on along his **beat**, trying doors as he went. [light fine rain]

[~about/of sth) feeling doubt about sth; not sure] [in a way that is steady and does not

There was now a fine, cold **drizzle**[5] falling, and the wind had risen from its uncertain puffs into a steady blow. The few foot passengers **astir**[6] [when the wind or a current of air blows, it is movin

in that quarter hurried **dismally**[7] and silently along with coat collars [causing or showing sadness] [the part around the neck,

turned high and pocketed hands. And in the door of the hardware store the man who had come a thousand miles to fill an appointment, uncertain almost to **absurdity**[8], with the friend of his youth, smoked his [the quality or state of being ridiculous or wholly unreasonable]

cigar and waited.

About twenty minutes he waited, and then a tall man in a long overcoat, with collar turned up to his ears, hurried across from the opposite side of the street. He went directly to the waiting man.

"Is that you, Bob?" he asked, doubtfully.

"Is that you, Jimmy Wells?" cried the man in the door.

"哎呀呀！"刚来的人也高声叫，一把抓起对方的两只手，"果然是鲍勃。我知道只要你还活着，一定会上这儿来。哟，哟，哟，二十年，可不算短呀！鲍勃，原来的餐馆已经没有了，要是还在多好，我们可以到里面再吃上一顿。在西部混得怎么样，老弟？"

"好极啦！我想到手的都到手了。吉米，你变了很多。奇怪，你怎么又长了两三寸呢？"

"是呀，满二十后我又长了些。"

"你在纽约怎么样，吉米？"

"还过得去。我在市政府谋了个位置。鲍勃，走吧，到一个我熟悉的地方去叙叙旧。"

两人手挽手沿马路走着。从西部归来的那个志得意满，讲起这些年的作为。另一个把头缩在大衣领里，津津有味地听着。

十字路口有家药房，仍灯火辉煌。到了灯光下，两人同时转身瞪大眼看着对方的脸。

从西部来的那个突然站住了，松开手臂。

"你不是吉米·韦尔斯！"他惊叫起来，"二十年的时间的确长，但再长的时间也不会把鹰钩鼻变成个扁鼻。"

"二十年足可以把一些好人变成坏人，"高个子说，"鲍勃，你已被捕十分钟了。芝加哥认为你可能上我们这儿来，打了电报说想与你谈谈。放老实点，知道吗？老实才聪明。有人叫我带张条子给你，看完了我们再去局里。你到那儿窗子

① moderately /ˈmɒdərɪtlɪ/ ad. 适度地,有节制地

② egotism /ˈeɡəʊtɪzəm/ n. 自我中心,自负
self-important
③ submerge /səbˈmɜːdʒ/ v. 潜入,淹没

④ drugstore /ˈdrʌɡstɔː/ n. 药店,杂货店

⑤ brilliant /ˈbrɪljənt/ a. 明亮

same 的 time as sth. else
⑥ simultaneously
/ˌsaɪməlˈteɪnɪəslɪ/ ad. 同时地
d. or because you are thinking of sth. else

attention to sb
⑦ wire /ˈwaɪə/ v. 打电报给

You may read it here at the window. It's from **Patrolman**[1] Wells."

The man from the West unfolded the little piece of paper handed him. His hand was steady when he began to read, but it trembled a little by the time he had finished. The note was rather short.

"Bob: I was at the appointed place on time. When you struck the match to light your cigar I saw it was the face of the man wanted in Chicago. Somehow I couldn't do it myself, so I went around and got a plain clothes man to do the job. JIMMY."

① patrolman /pə'trəulmən/
n. 巡警

[~ with sth.) to shake in a way
that you cannot control, especially
because you are very nervous,
excited, frightened, etc]

下看，是韦尔斯巡警写的。"

从西部来的人打开交给他的小纸条。开始看的时候他的手还正常，但到看完时却抖得厉害。条子上只写了几句话：

鲍勃：我准时到了约定地点。你划着火柴点烟时我发现你原来是芝加哥通缉的罪犯。我不忍自己动手，便找了位便衣代劳。吉米。

这篇小说真正触动我们的，恐怕是它背后的那个故事。

　　有人坚信奋斗可以帮助自己改变命运，另一些人则将感情视为他们残存于世的唯一理由，但是，当命运偏偏与他们作对时，也就是悲惨人生的开始了。

The Furnished Room

Restless, shifting, **fugacious**[1] as time itself is a certain vast bulk of the population of the red brick district of the lower West Side. Homeless, they have a hundred homes. They flit from furnished room to furnished room, **transients**[2] forever — transients in abode, transients in heart and mind. They sing "Home, Sweet Home" in ragtime; they carry their lares et penates in a bandbox; their vine is entwined about a picture hat; a rubber plant is their fig tree.

Hence the houses of this district, having had a thousand dwellers, should have a thousand tales to tell, mostly dull ones, no doubt; but it would be strange if there could not be found a ghost or two **in the wake of**[3] all these **vagrant**[4] guests.

One evening after dark a young man **prowled**[5] among these **crumbling**[6] red **mansions**[7], ringing their bells. At the twelfth he rested his lean hand-baggage upon the step and wiped the dust from his hatband and forehead. The bell sounded faint and far away in some remote, hollow depths.

To the door of this, the twelfth house whose bell he had rung, came a housekeeper who made him think of an unwholesome, **surfeited**[8]

带家具的房间

① fugacious /fjuːˈgeɪʃəs/ a. 短暂的

② transient /ˈtrænʃənt/ n. 短暂居住者;过往旅客

③ in the wake of 紧紧跟随……,在……后

④ vagrant /ˈveɪɡrənt/ a. 流浪的,漂泊不定的

⑤ prowl /praʊl/ v. 潜行,搜寻

⑥ crumble /ˈkrʌmbl/ v. 粉碎,弄碎

⑦ mansion /ˈmænʃən/ n. 公馆,宅第

⑧ surfeit /ˈsɜːfɪt/ v. 暴饮暴食

下西区有一片红砖楼,住在楼里的一大帮房客像时间一样永不停步,来去匆匆。他们处处无家,处处为家,从这间带家具的房间搬到那间带家具的房间,永远只是过客——不但住所无定,而且心绪、思想无定。他们和着散拍唱《家,幸福的家》;他们的家神是搁在纸盒里提来提去的;他们没有葡萄藤,只是帽子上绕着装饰带,也没有无花果树,只有盆景。

所以这一带房子里住过的房客上千,有的说的事也该上千。当然,大多数索然无味。不过,如果说这帮匆匆过客连一两件奇闻也没有,那又不可思议。

一天天黑以后,一位年轻人在这片破败的红砖房中走家串户,按着门铃。来到第十二栋后,他把寒酸的手提包放在台阶上,掸去帽带上的灰,又揩揩额头。铃声很轻,仿佛从隔得远远的、空荡荡的纵深处传来。

这一家(就是他按了铃的第十二家)的女房东来开了门,他一见不由想起了一条害虫,蛀光

worm that had eaten its nut to a hollow shell and now sought to fill the **vacancy**[1] with **edible**[2] **lodgers**[3].

He asked if there was a room to **let**[4].

"Come in," said the housekeeper. Her voice came from her throat; her throat seemed lined with fur. "I have the third floor back, vacant since a week back. Should you wish to look at it?"

The young man followed her up the stairs. A faint light from no particular source **mitigated**[5] the shadows of the halls. They trod noiselessly upon a stair carpet that its own loom would have forsworn. It seemed to have become vegetable; to have degenerated in that rank, sunless air to lush lichen or spreading moss that grew in patches to the staircase and was viscid under the foot like **organic**[6] matter. At each turn of the stairs were vacant niches in the wall. Perhaps plants had once been set within them. If so they had died in that foul and tainted air. It may be that statues of the saints had stood there, but it was not difficult to conceive that imps and **devils**[7] had dragged them forth in the darkness and down to the unholy depths of some furnished pit below.

"This is the room," said the housekeeper, from her furry throat. "It's a nice room. It ain't often vacant. I had some most elegant people in it last summer — no trouble at all, and paid in advance to the minute. The water's at the end of the hall. Sprowls and Mooney kept it three months. They done a vaudeville **sketch**[8]. Miss B'retta Sprowls — you may have heard of her — Oh, that was just the stage names — right there over the dresser is where the marriage certificate hung, **framed**[9]. The gas is here, and you see there is plenty of closet room. It's a room everybody likes. It never stays idle long."

"Do you have many theatrical people rooming here?" asked the young man.

① vacancy /'veɪkənsɪ/ n. 空白,空缺

② edible /'edɪbl/ a. 可食的,食用的

③ lodger /'lɒdʒə/ n. 房客

④ let /let/ v. 出租

⑤ mitigate /'mɪtɪgeɪt/ v. 减轻

⑥ organic /ɔːˈɡænɪk/ a. 器官的,有机体的

⑦ devil /'devl/ n. 魔鬼,恶魔

⑧ sketch /sketʃ/ n. 速写,草图

⑨ frame /freɪm/ v. 给……加框

了果仁,已经吃饱了撑着,可还巴望有房客送上门来给她塞塞牙缝。

他问有没有空房间。

"进来吧,"女房东说。她的声音是从喉管里发出的,而且喉管上似乎长了层苔,"三楼靠后有一间,还刚空了一星期,你去看看吧。"

年轻人跟她上了楼。不知从什么地方发出的微光照着黑乎乎的过道。两人的脚踩在楼梯的地毯上没一点声音,恐怕原来织出这块地毯的织机也认不出这块地毯了。它已面目全非,在有股臭味、不见阳光的空气中腐烂,变成青苔地衣似的东西,在楼梯上一块块扎了根,踩上去还粘脚,像是踩着了什么黏性强的有机物。在楼梯每个拐弯处的墙上都有壁龛,只是空着。也许壁龛里原摆过什么花草,然而禁不住又脏又臭的空气熏都已死绝。还有一种可能是摆过什么神像,但不难想象,大小魔鬼趁屋子里黑,把它们拖进了罪恶的深渊,让它们待在堆放家具的地窖里了。

"就是这一间,"女房东长了层苔的喉咙说,"房间挺好,并不常空着,夏天还住过几位贵客。都是痛快人,到时就预付房租。水在走廊那头。斯普罗尔斯与穆尼住过三个月。他们是演杂耍的。那位布雷特·斯普罗尔斯小姐——你总该听说过她吧?哦,对,那是她的艺名。她把结婚证配了个镜框,就挂在梳妆台上方。气灯在这里。你看,壁柜多大。这间房人人喜欢,从没有久空过。"

"当演员的人常到你这儿来住?"年轻人问。

"They comes and goes. A good proportion of my lodgers is connected with the theatres. Yes, sir, this is the theatrical district. Actor people never stays long anywhere. I get my share. Yes, they comes and they goes."

He engaged the room, paying for a week in advance. He was tired, he said, and would take possession at once. He counted out the money. The room had been made ready, she said, even to towels and water. As the housekeeper moved away he put, for the thousandth time, the question that he carried at the end of his tongue.

"A young girl — Miss Vashner — Miss Eloise Vashner — do you remember such a one among your lodgers? She would be singing on the stage, most likely. A fair girl, of medium height and slender, with reddish, gold hair and a dark mole near her left eyebrow."

"No, I don't remember the name. Them stage people has names they change as often as their rooms. They comes and they goes. No, I don't call that one to mind."

No. Always no. Five months of ceaseless **interrogation**[1] and the **inevitable**[2] negative. So much time spent by day in questioning managers, agents, schools and choruses; by night among the audiences of theatres from all-star casts down to music halls so low that he dreaded to find what he most hoped for. He who had loved her best had tried to find her. He was sure that since her disappearance from home this great, water-girt city held her somewhere, but it was like a monstrous quicksand, shifting its particles constantly, with no foundation, its upper granules of to-day buried to-morrow in **ooze**[3] and **slime**[4].

The furnished room received its latest guest with a first glow of

"来来去去的。上这儿的房客有一大半与剧场有关系。先生，你不知道，这一带就是剧院区。当演员的人从来就不在哪个地方久住。上我这儿的当然有。他们有来的，有去的，就这样。"

他租下了房间，预付一个星期租金。他说已经累了，想马上休息。钱如数交清。女房东告诉他，房间里什么都是现成的，连毛巾和水都已准备好。她正要转身走，年轻人问了一个问题。这个问题他已经问过一千遍了。

"你是不是记得房客里有个年轻姑娘？叫瓦什纳小姐，全名是埃勒威兹·瓦什纳。她很可能在登台演唱。是个漂亮姑娘，中等个子，身材苗条，头发深金黄色，左眼皮附近有颗黑痣。"

"这个名字我想不起来。他们当演员的今天住这间房明天住那间房，也今天叫这个名字明天叫那个名字。他们来的来，去的去。你说的名字我当真想不起来。"

白问，每次都白问，他不厌其烦地问了五个月，得到的回答都是不知道。白天花大气力找剧场经理、中介人、学校、歌舞团打听；夜晚在观众中转，从全是明星登台的大剧院直跑到下三流的音乐厅，连最怕在那儿找到朝思暮想的人的场所都不放过。他真心爱她，在千方百计找她。他相信，自离家出走后，她一定还在这座被水环抱的大城市的某个地方，只不过这座城市像一大片永无安稳之日的流沙，其中的沙粒不停地翻动，今天浮在表面的，明天又埋进淤泥里。

① interrogation
/ɪnˌterəˈɡeɪʃən/ n. 讯问，审问

② inevitable /ɪnˈevɪtəbl/ a. 不可避免的

③ ooze /uːz/ n. 沼泽，沼地

④ slime /slaɪm/ n. 黏泥，黏土

pseudo-hospitality, a **hectic**①, **haggard**②, **perfunctory**③ welcome like the specious smile of a demirep. The sophistical comfort came in reflected gleams from the decayed furniture, the raggcd brocade **upholstery**④ of a couch and two chairs, a footwide cheap pier glass between the two windows, from one or two gilt picture frames and a brass bedstead in a corner.

The guest reclined, inert, upon a chair, while the room, confused in speech as though it were an apartment in Babel, tried to discourse to him of its diverse tenantry.

A **polychromatic**⑤ rug like some brilliant-flowered rectangular, tropical islet lay surrounded by a billowy sea of soiled matting. Upon the gay-papered wall were those pictures that pursue the homeless one from house to house — The Huguenot Lovers, The First Quarrel, The Wedding Breakfast, Psyche at the Fountain. The mantel's chastely severe outline was ingloriously veiled behind some **pert**⑥ **drapery**⑦ drawn **rakishly**⑧ **askew**⑨ like the sashes of the Amazonian ballet. Upon it was some desolate **flotsam**⑩ cast aside by the room's marooned when a lucky sail had borne them to a fresh port — a trifling vase or two, pictures of actresses, a medicine bottle, some stray cards out of a deck.

One by one, as the characters of a cryptograph become explicit, the little signs left by the furnished room's procession of guests developed a significance. The threadbare space in the rug in front of the dresser told that lovely woman had marched in the throng. Tiny finger prints on the wall spoke of little prisoners trying to feel their way to sun and air. A **splattered**⑪ stain, raying like the shadow of a bursting bomb, witnessed where a **hurled**⑫ glass or bottle had splintered with its contents against the wall. Across the pier glass had been **scrawled**⑬ with a diamond in

① hectic /'hektɪk/ a. 兴奋
的,忙乱的

② haggard /'hægəd/ a. 憔悴
的,形容枯槁的

③ perfunctory /pə'fʌŋktərɪ/
a. 敷衍的,马虎的

④ upholstery /ʌp'həulstərɪ/
n. 室内装潢品,(沙发等
的)垫衬物

⑤ polychromatic
/pɒlɪkrəu'mætɪk/ a. 色彩
变化的

⑥ pert /pɜːt/ a. 雅致的,时髦
的

⑦ drapery /'dreɪpərɪ/ n. 布
匹,纺织品

⑧ rakishly /'reɪkɪʃlɪ/ ad. 浪
荡地,放荡地

⑨ askew /ə'skjuː/ a. 歪斜的

⑩ flotsam /'flɒtsəm/ n. （遇
难船只的）漂浮残骸

⑪ splatter /'splætə/ v. 溅泼,
溅湿

⑫ hurl /hɜːl/ v. (猛力)投掷

⑬ scrawl /skrɔːl/ v. 潦草地
写(或画)

起初，带家具的房间对它的新客来了一番假热情，那是一种看来激动、热烈，其实却虚应世故的欢迎，就像娼妓虚情假意的笑。旧家具还有反光；一张床、两把椅上蒙着破织锦；两扇窗之间有一面一尺宽的廉价穿衣镜；墙角里搁着一两个描金画框，一副铜床架等等，这使他或多或少觉得还不坏。

客人有气无力地往椅上一靠。顿时，他像进了通天塔，只听见操各种不同语言的人抢着告诉他这儿住过什么房客，简直乱成一团。

邋里邋遢的地席上铺着一方颜色杂七杂八的毯子，好似波涛汹涌的海洋中露出一个鲜花怒放的方形小岛。墙上糊着花花绿绿的墙纸，贴着无家无室的人在哪间客房都能看到的画，有《法国信新教的情侣》《首次口角》《新婚早餐》和《赛克在泉边》。壁炉前歪吊着块本来还成样子的布，就像歌剧中亚马孙人身上随便缠着根宽带子。壁炉朴实而庄严的轮廓被盖住了。壁炉上放着些乱七八糟的东西，有一两只不值钱的花瓶，几张女演员像，一只药瓶，几张零星纸牌，都是以前的房客留下的。那些人原先也落难到这荒岛，后来遇到别的船相救，人到新的港口登了岸，乱七八糟的东西就还留在荒岛上。

渐渐地，原先的房客留下的小物件让他看出了名堂，就像份密电码的字让他一个个破译了一样。梳妆台前的毯子上有一块地方磨光了毛，这说明许多漂亮女人在那儿踩过。墙上留着小手指印，那是小囚徒摸出来的，他们想见到阳光，呼吸新鲜空气。还留着一大块污渍，呈放射形，像

staggering letters the name "Marie." It seemed that the succession of dwellers in the furnished room had turned in fury — perhaps tempted beyond **forbearance**[1] by its **garish**[2] coldness — and **wreaked**[3] upon it their passions. The furniture was chipped and bruised; the couch, distorted by bursting springs, seemed a horrible monster that had been slain during the stress of some grotesque convulsion. Some more potent **upheaval**[4] had **cloven**[5] a great slice from the marble mantel. Each plank in the floor owned its particular cant and shriek as from a separate and individual agony. It seemed incredible that all this malice and injury had been wrought upon the room by those who had called it for a time their home; and yet it may have been the cheated home instinct surviving blindly, the resentful rage at false household gods that had kindled their wrath. A hut that is our own we can sweep and adorn and cherish.

The young tenant in the chair allowed these thoughts to file, soft-shod, through his mind, while there drifted into the room furnished sounds and furnished scents. He heard in one room a **tittering**[6] and incontinent, slack laughter; in others the monologue of a scold, the rattling of dice, a lullaby, and one crying dully; above him a **banjo**[7] tinkled with spirit. Doors banged somewhere; the elevated trains roared intermittently; a cat yowled miserably upon a back fence. And he breathed the breath of the house — a dank savour rather than a smell — a cold, musty **effluvium**[8] as from underground **vaults**[9] mingled with the reeking **exhalations**[10] of **linoleum**[11] and mildewed and rotten woodwork.

Then, suddenly, as he rested there, the room was filled with the strong, sweet odour of mignonette. It came as upon a single buffet of

① forbearance /fɔːˈbeərəns/
n. 忍耐

② garish /ˈɡeərɪʃ/ a. 过分鲜
艳的,耀眼的

③ wreak /riːk/ v. 发泄

④ upheaval /ʌpˈhiːvəl/ n. 动
乱,激变,剧变

⑤ cloven /ˈklʌvən/ v. 砍出,
劈出。cleave的过去分词

⑥ titter /ˈtɪtə/ v. 吃吃地笑,
偷笑

⑦ banjo /ˈbændʒəu/ n. 五弦
琴

⑧ effluvium /eˈfluːvɪəm/ n.
臭气

⑨ vault /vɔːlt/ n. 拱顶,地窖

⑩ exhalation /ˌekshəˈleɪʃən/
n. 呼气,蒸发,散发

⑪ linoleum /lɪˈnəʊlɪəm/ n.
亚麻油地毡,铺地板油布

炸弹开花,显然是有人把一杯或者一瓶什么东西往墙上一甩甩出来的。穿衣镜让人用金刚石横着歪歪扭扭刻了个名字:玛丽。看来,以往的房客一个个都有股子火气(也许是受不住这儿虚情假意的冷漠发了火),一怒之下便把房间当出气筒。家具已被弄得遍体鳞伤。床上的弹簧东一个西一个冒了出来,整个床便不成样子,活像只死于恶性痉挛的大怪物。壁炉上的大理石不知由于出了什么大乱子,被敲掉了一大块。地板上的每块木板各有各的伤痛,因为各自受过各自的冤屈。那些房客暂住这房间时都暂以这房间为家,却又产生这么多怨气,进行这么多破坏,真难以想象。但也许正由于他们需要家的天性没有真正泯灭却又不得满足,由于他们对冒牌家切齿痛恨,一腔怒火才烧了起来。只要真是自己家,哪怕一间茅棚,我们都会打扫、装饰、爱惜。

年轻房客靠在椅子上,任凭脑海里的思绪一个接一个飘过。飘着飘着,他听到了别的房间里传来的声音,嗅到了别的房间传来的气味。有人在淫荡地吃吃笑,有人在不绝口地骂,有人在骨碌碌掷骰子,有人在哼催眠曲,有人抽抽噎噎哭,只听楼上又传来一阵欢快的五弦琴声。还有乒乒乓乓的门响,高架铁路上一趟一趟的火车叫,后围墙上凄厉的猫嚎。他嗅出了屋子里的味不是一股正常气味,而是一股发潮的怪味,冷飕飕,带霉臭,像是堆放油布和霉变、发烂的木制品的地下室里发出的。

他靠着没动,突然又闻到一股浓郁的木樨草香,像是一阵风送来的,直扑鼻孔,他闻得十分真

wind with such sureness and fragrance and emphasis that it almost seemed a living **visitant**①. And the man cried aloud: "What, dear?" as if he had been called, and sprang up and faced about. The rich **odor**② clung to him and wrapped him around. He reached out his arms for it, all his s enses for the time confused and **commingled** ③. How could one be **peremptorily**④ called by an odour? Surely it must have been a sound. But, was it not the sound that had touched, that had caressed him?

"She has been in this room," he cried, and he sprang to wrest from it a token, for he knew he would recognize the smallest thing that had belonged to her or that she had touched. This enveloping scent of mignonette, the odour that she had loved and made her own — **whence**⑤ came it?

The room had been but carelessly set in order. Scattered upon the flimsy dresser scarf were half a dozen hairpins — those discreet, indistinguishable friends of womankind, **feminine**⑥ of gender, infinite of mood and uncommunicative of tense. These he ignored, conscious of their triumphant lack of identity. **Ransacking**⑦ the drawers of the dresser he came upon a discarded, tiny, ragged handkerchief. He pressed it to his face. It was racy and **insolent**⑧ with **heliotrope**⑨; he hurled it to the floor. In another drawer he found odd buttons, a theatre programme, a pawnbroker's card, two lost marshmallows, a book on the divination of dreams. In the last was a woman's black satin hair bow, which halted him, poised between ice and fire. But the black satin hairbow also is femininity's **demure**⑩, impersonal, common **ornament**⑪, and tells no tales.

And then he traversed the room like a hound on the scent, skimming the walls, considering the corners of the bulging matting on

切，就好比见到有血有肉的来客，错不了。年轻人似乎听到了有人叫唤，大声道："什么事，亲爱的？"他还一跃而起，往四周望着。浓郁的香味没有消退，萦绕在他前后左右。他竟然伸出手抓，一时间六神无主。香味怎么可能开口叫人呢？一定是听到了声音。但是声音怎么能摸他、抚弄他呢？

"她住过这房间！"他嚷了起来。又一纵身起来，想找出什么东西证实。他有把握，凡是归她所有的，甚至她碰过的东西，再小他也准能认出来。这股经久不绝的木樨草香是她喜爱的，也是她独有的，究竟从哪儿来的呢？

房间几乎没怎么收拾。梳妆台的薄台布上东一只西一只放着五六只发夹。发夹是哪个女人都少不了的朋友，含蓄内敛，什么也不会透露，就像一个仅属于阴性，但既不表示情态也没有时态变化的词。他没有细看，知道再看也看不出个名堂来。一翻梳妆台的抽屉，发现了一方小小的破手帕。他把手帕贴到脸上，闻到的是刺鼻的金盏草味，忙往地上一扔。在另一个抽屉里他发现了几粒纽扣，一张节目单，一张当铺老板的名片，两颗忘了吃的白软糖，一本解梦的书。书里夹着一根女人用的黑缎蝴蝶结，他一见愣住了，说不清是喜是悲。但黑缎蝴蝶结也是女人都用的装饰品，平平常常，不是谁所独有，说明不了问题。

接着他像猎狗嗅到什么气味般满房间乱窜，扫视墙壁，趴到地上察看地席隆起的地方，搜索壁炉、桌子、窗帘、吊着的挂着的东西、房角那个

① visitant /'vɪzɪtənt/ n. 访客，参观者
② odor /'əudə/ n. 气味
③ commingle /kə'mɪŋgl/ v. 掺和，混合
④ peremptorily /pə'remptərɪlɪ/ ad. 独断地，横蛮地

⑤ whence /hwens/ ad. 从何处

⑥ feminine /'femɪnɪn/ a. 女性的

⑦ ransack /'rænsæk/ v. 彻底搜索，仔细搜查

⑧ insolent /'ɪnsələnt/ a. 傲慢无礼的，粗野的
⑨ heliotrope /'heljətrəup/ n. 天芥菜属植物

⑩ demure /dɪ'mjuə/ a. 装作一本正经的，佯作害羞的
⑪ ornament /'ɔ:nəmənt/ n. 装饰品

his hands and knees, **rummaging**① mantel and tables, the curtains and hangings, the drunken cabinet in the corner, for a visible sign, unable to perceive that she was there beside, around, against, within, above him, clinging to him, wooing him, calling him so **poignantly**② through the finer senses that even his grosser ones became cognisant of the call. Once again he answered loudly: "Yes, dear! " and turned, wild-eyed, to gaze on vacancy, for he could not yet discern form and color and love and outstretched arms in the odor of **mignonette**③. Oh, God! Whence that odor, and since when have odors had a voice to call? Thus he groped.

He **burrowed**④ in **crevices**⑤ and corners, and found corks and cigarettes. These he passed in passive contempt. But once he found in a fold of the matting a half-smoked cigar, and this he ground beneath his heel with a green and trenchant oath. He sifted the room from end to end. He found dreary and ignoble small records of many a **peripatetic**⑥ tenant; but of her whom he sought, and who may have lodged there, and whose spirit seemed to hover there, he found no trace.

And then he thought of the housekeeper.

He ran from the haunted room downstairs and to a door that showed a crack of light. She came out to his knock. He smothered his excitement as best he could.

"Will you tell me, madam," he besought her, "who occupied the room I have before I came? "

"Yes, sir. I can tell you again. 'Twas Sprowls and Mooney, as I said. Miss B'retta Sprowls it was in the theatres, but Missis Mooney she was. My house is well known for respectability. The marriage certificate hung, framed, on a nail over — "

① rummage /'rʌmɪdʒ/ v. 仔
细搜查

② poignantly /'pɔɪɡnəntlɪ/ ad.
令人辛酸地;深刻地

③ mignonette /ˌmɪnjə'net/ n.
木犀草

④ burrow /'bʌrəʊ/ v. 挖通道,
深入搜寻

⑤ crevice /'krevɪs/ n. 裂缝,
裂隙

⑥ peripatetic /ˌperɪpə'tetɪk/
a. 流动的

放不稳的柜子,一心要找出点线索,却没发现她就在身边,在心头,在上空,在围着他转,在依偎着他,在搂着他,在追寻他,在冥冥中呼唤他,虽然无声,他这凡人的耳朵也听到了这凄惨的呼唤。他又一次大声应道:"在这里,亲爱的!"他一转身,大睁着眼,什么人也没有见到。他闻到的木犀草香味怎会有形,有色,会张开双手,会表示爱情呢?苍天在上,这股香味来自何方呢?香味怎么能发出声音叫唤呢?他又开始搜寻。

他找遍每一条缝隙,每一个角落,只找到了瓶塞、香烟。这些东西他不屑一顾。但有一次他在地席的折缝里发现一根抽了半截的烟,他把它塞到脚底下踩扁了,还恶狠狠骂了一声。他把整间房一寸一寸搜遍了。别的房客丢下的乌七八糟的小东西发现不少,但是他在找寻的那个人,那个很可能在这里住过,而且灵魂似乎仍在这里徘徊的人,却没见留下遗迹。

后来他想到了女房东。

他跑出闹鬼的房间,下了楼,走到一间露出亮光的房。女房东听到敲门声出来了。他极力抑制住自己的情绪。

"请问,我来前是谁住过这房间?"他问道。

"我就再告诉你一遍吧,先生。我说过了,是斯普罗尔斯与穆尼。她演出的时候叫布雷特·斯普罗尔斯小姐,其实是穆尼太太。我这房子可是有声誉的房子。结婚证还框在镜框里,挂在——"

"What kind of a lady was Miss Sprowls — in looks, I mean?"

"Why, black-haired, sir, short, and **stout**①, with a **comical**② face. They left a week ago Tuesday."

"And before they occupied it?"

"Why, there was a single gentleman connected with the draying business. He left owing me a week. Before him was Missis Crowder and her two children, that stayed four months; and back of them was old Mr. Doyle, whose sons paid for him. He kept the room six months. That goes back a year, sir, and further I do not remember."

He thanked her and crept back to his room. The room was dead. The **essence**③ that had **vivified**④ it was gone. The perfume of mignonette had departed. In its place was the old, stale odor of mouldy house furniture, of atmosphere in storage.

The **ebbing**⑤ of his hope **drained**⑥ his faith. He sat staring at the yellow, singing gaslight. Soon he walked to the bed and began to tear the sheets into strips. With the blade of his knife he drove them tightly into every crevice around windows and door. When all was **snug**⑦ and taut he turned out the light, turned the gas full on again and laid himself gratefully upon the bed.

* * * * * * *

It was Mrs. McCool's night to go with the can for beer. So she fetched it and sat with Mrs. Purdy in one of those **subterranean**⑧ retreats where house-keepers foregather and the worm dieth seldom.

"I rented out my third floor, back, this evening," said Mrs. Purdy, across a fine circle of **foam**⑨. "A young man took it. He went up to bed two hours ago."

"Now, did ye, Mrs. Purdy, ma'am?" said Mrs. McCool, with

① stout /staʊt/ a. 肥胖的，发胖的
② comical /'kɒmɪkəl/ a. 滑稽的，诙谐的

③ essence /'esns/ n. 实质，本体
④ vivify /'vɪvɪfaɪ/ v. （使）生动
⑤ ebbing /ebɪŋ/ n. 低落，衰退
⑥ drain /dreɪn/ v. 使逐渐消失
⑦ snug /snʌg/ a. 舒适的，温暖的

⑧ subterranean /ˌsʌbtə'reɪnɪən/ a. 地下的
⑨ foam /fəʊm/ n. 泡沫

"斯普罗尔斯小姐是怎么样个人？我是说她的长相。"

"你问这呀——长着黑头发，又矮又壮实，脸挺古怪。夫妻俩上星期二走的。"

"他们来之前呢？"

"是个单身男人，与车行打交道的。他还赖了我一星期房租没付。再往前数是克劳德太太带着两个孩子，住了四个月。他们来之前住的是多伊尔先生，一个老头，他的儿子轮流替他付房租。他住了半年。这样数数也就有一年时间了。再往前的我忘了，先生。"

他向她道了声谢，有气无力地回到自己房间。房间里死气沉沉。曾使他忙了好大一阵的东西没有了。木樨草的香味已经消失，闻到的是霉家具的陈腐气味，就是贮藏室的窒息气味。

希望的破灭使他失去了信心。他坐着眼望嘶嘶发响的黄煤气灯发呆。过了一会，他走到床边，把床单撕成了破布条，然后用小刀把破布条牢牢塞进门缝里和窗缝里，一条缝都没漏。做得万无一失后，他灭了灯，然后把煤气开足，往床上一躺，什么也不再想。

* * *

今晚轮到麦库尔太太打啤酒。她打上一罐啤酒，拿到地下室和帕迪太太聊天。这种地下室不同一般，常有好几位房东太太凑到一起，在这里，她们的馋虫从没消停的时候。

"今天晚上我三楼的后房租出去了。"帕迪太太说，摆在两人间的啤酒还有圈泡没消，"是个年轻人租的，他两小时前就睡了。"

intense admiration. "You do be a wonder for rentin' rooms of that kind. And did ye tell him, then? " she concluded in a husky whisper, laden with mystery.

"Rooms," said Mrs. Purdy, in her furriest tones, "are furnished for to rent. I did not tell him, Mrs. McCool."

"'Tis right ye are, ma'am; 'tis by renting rooms we kape alive. Ye have the rale sense for business, ma'am. There be many people will rayjict the rentin' of a room if they be tould a **suicide**[①] has been after dyin' in the bed of it."

"As you say, we has our living to be making," remarked Mrs. Purdy.

"Yis, ma'am; 'tis true. 'Tis just one wake ago this day I helped ye lay out the third floor, back. A pretty slip of a colleen she was to be killin' herself wid the gas — a swate little face she had, Mrs. Purdy, ma'am."

"She'd a-been called handsome, as you say," said Mrs. Purdy, assenting but critical, "but for that mole she had a-growin' by her left eyebrow. Do fill up your glass again, Mrs. McCool."

"这事当真，帕迪太太？"麦库尔太太问道，心里好生佩服，"那种房间还能租出去，你真有两下子。难道你对他说了实话？"她迷惑不解，最后忍不住轻声问，声音发哑。

"房间里配上家具就是为出租。我没有对他说实话，麦库尔太太。"帕迪太太那长了苔的喉管答话道。

"你说得有理，太太。我们过日子靠的就是租出去房间。太太你真在行。要是听说床上自杀①死过人，不肯租的人可多着呐。"

"你也说得对，我们总还得过日子。"帕迪太太说。

"太太，那可不？上个星期，也是这日子，我还帮你收拾了三楼的后房间。想不到那漂亮妞会开煤气自杀。帕迪太太，你看她的小脸多逗人爱。"

"你没说错，她也算得上个标致人儿，就可惜左眼皮上长坏了颗痣。"帕迪太太既赞同又挑了点刺，"麦库尔太太，再来一杯!"

① suicide /'sjuːisaid/ n. 自杀

典型的欧·亨利式情节。

这个神秘的姑娘到底是什么人？哈！看你怎样一步步被引入陷阱，到达一个出人意料的结尾。

"*Girl*"

In gilt letters on the ground glass of the door of room No. 962 were the words: "Robbins & Hartley, Brokers." The clerks had gone. It was past five, and with the solid **tramp**① of a drove of prize Percherons, scrub-women were **invading** ② the cloud-capped twenty-story office building. A puff of red-hot air flavored with lemon **peelings**③, soft-coal smoke and train oil came in through the half-open windows.

Robbins, fifty, something of an overweight beau, and addicted to first nights and hotel palm-rooms, pretended to be envious of his partner's commuter's joys.

"Going to be something doing in the **humidity**④ line to-night," he said. "You out-of-town chaps will be the people, with your katydids and moonlight and long drinks and things out on the front porch."

Hartley, twenty-nine, serious, thin, good-looking, nervous, sighed and **frowned**⑤ a little.

"Yes," said he, "we always have cool nights in Floralhurst, especially in the winter."

A man with an air of mystery came in the door and went up to Hartley.

"姑娘"

① tramp /træmp/ *n.* 沉重的脚步声

② invade /ɪn'veɪd/ *v.* 涌入，大批进入

③ peeling /'piːlɪŋ/ *n.* （削下的）皮，果皮

④ humidity /hjuː'mɪdɪtɪ/ *n.* 湿气，湿度

⑤ frown /fraʊn/ *v.* 皱眉

962号房间门上的毛玻璃上有几个描金字：经纪人罗宾斯、哈特利。办事员已经走了。这时已过五点，女清扫工进了这座云雾缭绕的二十层办公楼。她们走起路来步子沉重，抵得过一群法国珀什的良种马。一股热风扑面吹进半开的窗里，夹带着柠檬皮味，煤烟味，还有火车机油味。

罗宾斯年已五十，体重有些超重，穿得俏。他爱看首演，住宾馆要有棕榈的高档房间。他的伙伴住郊外，他倒装出羡慕郊外人的模样，说：

"今天晚上的天气有变化。还是你们在城外的人好，可以坐在门厅里，听虫叫，看月光，慢慢喝酒，欣赏大自然。"

哈特利二十九岁，不苟言笑，消瘦，长相好，精力饱满。他一叹气，一皱眉，说：

"可是我们住弗洛勒尔赫斯特的人夜晚冷飕飕，尤其在冬天。"

这时一个神态诡秘的人打开门直走到哈特利身边。

"I've found where she lives," he announced in the **portentous**①
half-whisper that makes the detective at work a marked being to his
fellow men.

Hartley scowled him into a state of dramatic silence and quietude.
But by that time Robbins had got his cane and set his tie pin to his
liking, and with a **debonair**② nod went out to his **metropolitan**③
amusements.

"Here is the address," said the detective in a natural tone, being
deprived④ of an audience to foil.

Hartley took the leaf torn out of the **sleuth**⑤'s dingy memorandum
book. On it were **pencilled**⑥ the words "Vivienne Arlington, No. 341
East – – th Street, care of Mrs. McComus."

"Moved there a week ago," said the detective. "Now, if you want
any shadowing done, Mr. Hartley, I can do you as fine a job in that line
as anybody in the city. It will be only $7 a day and expenses. Can send
in a daily typewritten report, covering — "

"You needn't go on," interrupted the broker. "It isn't a case of that
kind. I merely wanted the address. How much shall I pay you? "

"One day's work," said the sleuth. "A tenner will cover it."

Hartley paid the man and dismissed him. Then he left the office and
boarded a Broadway car. At the first large crosstown **artery**⑦ of travel he
took an eastbound car that deposited him in a **decaying**⑧ avenue, whose
ancient structures once sheltered the pride and glory of the town.

Walking a few squares, he came to the building that he sought. It
was a new flathouse, bearing carved upon its cheap stone portal its
sonorous⑨ name, "The Vallambrosa." Fire-escapes zigzagged down its
front — these laden with household goods, drying clothes, and squalling

① portentous /pɔːˈtentəs/ a.
自命不凡的,自负的

② debonair /ˌdebəˈneə (r)/ a.
温文有礼的

③ metropolitan
/ˌmetrəˈpɒlɪtən/ a.大都市
的

④ deprive /dɪˈpraɪv/ v. 剥
夺,使丧失

⑤ sleuth /sluːθ/ n.〈口〉侦探

⑥ pencil /ˈpensl/ v. 用铅笔
写(或画)

⑦ artery /ˈɑːtərɪ/ n. 干线,要
道

⑧ decay /dɪˈkeɪ/ v. 腐朽,腐
烂

⑨ sonorous /səˈnɔːrəs/ a. 作
响的,能发出响亮声音的

"我打听到她的住址啦。"这位侦探轻声而得意扬扬地说,惹得在场的人都把注意力转向他。

哈特利把脸一沉,侦探马上闭上了嘴没出声。但这时罗宾斯已拿起了手杖,把领带别针别到了理想位置。他彬彬有礼地一点头,出门享受他的大城市的乐趣去了。

"她的住址在这儿。"侦探见没有人听他炫耀了,声音变自然了。

哈特利从侦探的脏记事本上撕下一页,上面用铅笔写着:"维维恩,东第××大街341号,麦科默斯太太转。"

"上星期搬去的。"侦探说,"哈特利先生,如果你需要跟踪,我会干得漂漂亮亮,跟全市吃这行饭的人谁都能比。价钱每天只七元,其他开销除外。天天有打字机打的书面报告,包括……"

经纪人打断他的话:"你不用再说了。不是那种事。我仅仅需要个地址。多少钱?"

"一天工夫,"侦探说,"十元够了。"

哈特利付过钱后打发走了来人。然后他也离开办公室,坐上了去百老汇的车。到了第一条穿城交通大动脉,他改乘一辆往东的车,坐到一条已经破落的老街,往日这儿的古老建筑曾是全市的骄傲和光荣。

没走多远,他找到了要找的341号。原来,是一所新建的公寓,廉价石头砌的前门上刻着房子的响亮的名字:瓦勒姆布罗瑟。曲曲拐拐的太平梯建在正面,上面挂着日用杂品,晾着衣服,还趴着些孩子在喊喊叫叫,他们是受不住盛夏的炎热跑出屋子来的。在这些乱七八糟的东西中东零

children evicted by the midsummer heat. Here and there a pale rubber plant peeped from the **miscellaneous**① mass, as if wondering to what kingdom it belonged — vegetable, animal or artificial.

Hartley pressed the "McComus" button. The door latch clicked **spasmodically**② — now hospitably, now doubtfully, as though in anxiety whether it might be admitting friends or duns. Hartley entered and began to climb the stairs after the manner of those who seek their friends in city flat-houses — which is the manner of a boy who climbs an apple-tree, stopping when he comes upon what he wants.

On the fourth floor he saw Vivienne standing in an open door. She invited him inside, with a nod and a bright, genuine smile. She placed a chair for him near a window, and poised herself gracefully upon the edge of one of those **Jekyll-and-Hyde**③ pieces of furniture that are masked and mysteriously **hooded**④, unguessable bulks by day and **inquisitorial**⑤ racks of torture by night.

Hartley cast a quick, critical, appreciative glance at her before speaking, and told himself that his taste in choosing had been flawless.

Vivienne was about twenty-one. She was of the purest Saxon type. Her hair was a **ruddy**⑥ golden, each **filament**⑦ of the neatly gathered mass shining with its own lustre and delicate graduation of color. In perfect harmony were her ivory-clear complexion and deep sea-blue eyes that looked upon the world with the ingenuous calmness of a **mermaid**⑧ or the **pixie**⑨ of an undiscovered mountain stream. Her frame was strong and yet possessed the grace of absolute naturalness. And yet with all her Northern clearness and frankness of line and coloring, there seemed to be something of the tropics in her — something of **languor**⑩ in the droop of her pose, of love of ease in her ingenious complacency of satisfaction and comfort in the mere act of breathing — something that seemed to

① miscellaneous
/ˌmɪsə'leɪnjəs/ a. 混杂的，
五花八门的

② spasmodically
/spæz'mɒdɪkəlɪ/ ad. 断续
性地

③ Jekyll-an-Hyde 出自英国
作家史蒂文森的作品《化
身博士》，双重人格的代称

④ hood /hʊd/ v. 给……罩上
兜帽(或风帽)

⑤ inquisitorial
/ɪnˌkwɪzɪ'tɔːrɪəl/ a. 审判
官(似)的

⑥ ruddy /'rʌdɪ/ a. 红润的，
气色好的

⑦ filament /'fɪləmənt/ n. 细
丝，细线

⑧ mermaid /'mɜːmeɪd/ n. 美
人鱼

⑨ pixie /'pɪksɪ/ n. 小妖精，
小精灵

⑩ languor /'læŋɡə/ n. 倦怠

西散还可见到些营养不良的橡胶树在探头探脑，仿佛它们不知道自己居于什么王国——植物王国？动物王国？还是用品王国？

哈特利按了麦科默斯家的门铃。门锁嘎嘎嘎响着开了，既有热情，也带怀疑，似乎急着要瞧瞧来的人是朋友还是债主。哈特利进门后往楼上走。他与所有在城市的公寓里找朋友的人一样，或者说与爬苹果树的孩子一样，遇上他想要的一个才停下来。

在四楼他看到了维维恩，正站在一扇开着的门边。她点点头，开朗、真诚地一笑，把他请进了房，搬了张椅子放在窗边让他坐。自己却优雅地往家具边一靠。这些家具白天被遮盖着不露真面目，是个猜不透的庞然大物，夜晚却像拷问口供的刑具台，有两副模样。

哈特利先用敏锐的、欣赏的目光扫了她一眼才开口，心中暗想，他眼力不坏，还从没出过差错。

维维恩二十一岁上下，纯正典型的撒克逊人。头发金里透红，整整齐齐盘在头上，每根都有它独特的光泽，每根的颜色都由浅渐深。雪白的皮肤与海水般深蓝的眼睛交相辉映。两只眼看什么都不慌不忙，使人想起美人鱼或者人迹罕至的深山小溪中的小精灵。体格结实而身材各部分匀称协调。从轮廓与肤色看她显而易见是北方人，但她同时又显现出了热带地方人的一些特征：动作略显慵懒，神态从容不迫，似乎无忧无虑，连呼吸都分外节奏均匀。她使人感到她不愧是大自然的一件杰作，像一朵珍奇的花，像立在一群杂色

claim for her a right as a perfect work of nature to exist and be admired equally with a rare flower or some beautiful, milk-white dove among its sober-hued companions.

She was dressed in a white waist and dark skirt — that discreet **masquerade**[①] of goose-girl and duchess.

"Vivienne," said Hartley, looking at her pleadingly, "you did not answer my last letter. It was only by nearly a week's search that I found where you had moved to. Why have you kept me in **suspense**[②] when you knew how anxiously I was waiting to see you and hear from you? "

The girl looked out the window dreamily.

"Mr. Hartley," she said hesitatingly, "I hardly know what to say to you. I realize all the advantages of your offer, and sometimes I feel sure that I could be contented with you. But, again, I am doubtful. I was born a city girl, and I am afraid to bind myself to a quiet suburban life."

"My dear girl," said Hartley, **ardently**[③], "have I not told you that you shall have everything that your heart can desire that is in my power to give you? You shall come to the city for the theatres, for shopping and to visit your friends as often as you care to. You can trust me, can you not? "

"To the fullest," she said, turning her frank eyes upon him with a smile. "I know you are the kindest of men, and that the girl you get will be a lucky one. I learned all about you when I was at the Montgomerys'."

"Ah! " exclaimed Hartley, with a tender, reminiscent light in his eye; "I remember well the evening I first saw you at the Montgomerys'. Mrs. Montgomery was sounding your praises to me all the evening. And she hardly did you justice. I shall never forget that supper. Come,

鸽子中的一只美丽的洁白的鸽子，叫人爱慕不已。

她上穿白色开胸衣，下系黑裙，这身不事张扬的打扮既像是在饰演牧鹅姑娘，也像是在饰演公爵夫人。

"维维恩，"哈特利说，眼里现出恳求的神情，"我上次给你的信你没回。我花了将近一个星期时间才找到你的新住址。你知道我想见到你，看到你的回信，你为什么要让我等得心焦呢？"

姑娘茫然望着窗外。

"哈特利先生，"她有些犹豫，只是说，"我不知道说什么好。我完全清楚你提的事的好处，有时候也觉得跟你在一起会心满意足。可是我仍不敢确定。我是城市生城市长的人，怕是受不了长期过安静的乡下生活。"

哈特利热情地说："我的好姑娘，不是对你说了吗，你想要什么，只要我力所能及，都会满足你的要求。你可以到城里上剧院，买东西，看朋友，跑多少趟随你的便。你可以信得过我，不是吗？"

她回头一笑，用坦率的目光望着他，说："当然相信。我知道你这人心最好，哪个姑娘到你那儿都要算是有福气。在蒙哥马利家时我就把你的为人了解得清清楚楚了。"

"对！"哈特利大声道，眼里透出了柔情，心里回忆着往事，"在蒙哥马利家第一次见到你的那个夜晚我还记忆犹新。蒙哥马利太太不停地对我夸奖你，可你比她说的还要好。我永远忘不了那顿晚餐。维维恩，听我说，你答应我吧。我需要你。你

① masquerade /ˌmæskəˈreɪd/ n. 假面舞会，伪装

② suspense /səˈspens/ n. 挂虑，悬念

③ ardently /ˈɑːdntlɪ/ ad. 热心地

Vivienne, promise me. I want you. You'll never regret coming with me. No one else will ever give you as pleasant a home."

The girl sighed and looked down at her folded hands.

A sudden jealous **suspicion**① seized Hartley.

"Tell me, Vivienne," he asked, regarding her keenly, "is there another — is there someone else ? "

A rosy **flush**② crept slowly over her fair cheeks and neck.

"You shouldn't ask that, Mr. Hartley," she said, in some confusion. "But I will tell you. There is one other — but he has no right — I have promised him nothing."

"His name? " demanded Hartley, sternly.

"Townsend."

"Rafford Townsend! " exclaimed Hartley, with a grim tightening of his jaw. "How did that man come to know you? After all I've done for him — "

"His auto has just stopped below," said Vivienne, bending over the window-sill. "He's coming for his answer. Oh I don't know what to do! "

The bell in the flat kitchen **whirred**③. Vivienne hurried to press the latch button.

"Stay here," said Hartley. "I will meet him in the hall."

Townsend, looking like a Spanish **grandee**④ in his light **tweeds**⑤, Panama hat and curling black mustache, came up the stairs three at a time. He stopped at sight of Hartley and looked foolish.

"Go back," said Hartley, firmly, pointing downstairs with his forefinger.

"Hullo! " said Townsend, **feigning**⑥ surprise. "What's up? What are you doing here, old man? "

跟我走绝不会后悔的。别人谁也不能使你有这么个称心如意的家。"

姑娘叹口气，低头看着自己交叉放着的一双手。

哈特利突然起了怀疑，心里酸溜溜的。

他紧紧盯着她，问道："维维恩，你说实话，是不是还——还有什么人？"

① suspicion /səs'pɪʃən/ n. 怀疑心，猜疑

她雪白的脸上慢慢地泛起一阵红晕，直红到耳根。

② flush /flʌʃ/ n. 兴奋，激动

"哈特利先生，你这话问得不应该，"姑娘说，心有些乱，"不过我可以对你说。的确还有一个，但他不能够——我什么也没答应他。"

"他姓什么？"哈特利厉声追问道。

"汤森。"

"拉福特·汤森！"哈特利大声道，脸和下巴都拉长了，"怎么那家伙会认识你？我为他帮了那么多忙，可是他……"

维维恩把身子探出窗外，说："他的车说来就来了。他等着我答复。糟啦，我怎么办呢？"

③ whir /hwɜː/ v. 呼呼作声地飞（或转）

厨房里的铃一个劲儿地响着。维维恩赶忙去按前门的门闩钮。

④ grandee /græn'diː/ n. 大人物，显要人物

"你就在这里，等我去走廊对付他。"哈特利说。

⑤ tweeds /twiːdz/ n.（粗）花呢粗装

汤森穿着浅色苏格兰粗呢衣，头戴巴拿马帽，上唇的黑胡须向上翻卷，活像西班牙贵族，正三步并作两步地上楼来。他一见哈特利，傻了眼。

"快回去！"哈特利手指着楼下，厉声说。

⑥ feign /feɪn/ v. 装作，假装

"你好！"汤森假装意外，说，"这是怎么啦？什么风把你吹来啦，老兄？"

"Go back," repeated Hartley, inflexibly. "The Law of the Jungle. Do you want the Pack to tear you in pieces? The **kill**[1] is mine."

"I came here to see a plumber about the bathroom connections," said Townsend, bravely.

"All right," said Hartley. "You shall have that lying plaster to stick upon your traitorous soul. But, go back." Townsend went downstairs, leaving a bitter word to be **wafted**[2] up the draught of the **staircase**[3]. Hartley went back to his **wooing**[4].

"Vivienne," said he, masterfully. "I have got to have you. I will take no more refusals or **dilly-dallying**[5]."

"When do you want me? " she asked.

"Now. As soon as you can get ready."

She stood calmly before him and looked him in the eye.

"Do you think for one moment," she said, "that I would enter your home while Heloise is there? "

Hartley **cringed**[6] as if from an unexpected blow. He folded his arms and paced the carpet once or twice.

"She shall go," he declared grimly. Drops stood upon his brow. "Why should I let that woman make my life **miserable**[7]? Never have I seen one day of freedom from trouble since I have known her. You are right, Vivienne. Heloise must be sent away before I can take you home. But she shall go. I have decided. I will turn her from my doors."

"When will you do this? " asked the girl.

Hartley **clinched**[8] his teeth and bent his brows together.

"To-night," he said, resolutely. "I will send her away to-night."

"Then," said Vivienne, "my answer is 'yes.' Come for me when you will."

She looked into his eyes with a sweet, sincere light in her own.

① kill /kɪl/ n. 猎物

"快回去！"哈特利毫不含糊地又说道，"强者为王！难道你还想敲断脊梁骨不成？这儿我当道！"

汤森也有胆量，说："我来这儿是请管道工修浴室的接头。"

"那行呀！"哈特利说，"你这臭小子撒谎就不怕掉舌头！还是快回去吧。"汤森只好下楼，骂了一句算是对楼梯上的人的报复。哈特利回到房里又继续恳求。

② waft /wɑːft/ v. 随风传送
③ staircase /'steəkeɪs/ n. 楼梯，楼梯间
④ wooing /wuːɪŋ/ n. 央求，努力说服
⑤ dilly-dallying /'dɪlɪdælɪŋ/ n. 犹豫

"维维恩，我是非要你不可。你不答应不行，拖时间也不行。"他说，没留回旋的余地。

"你什么时候要我？"她问。

"现在，你收拾好就行。"

她镇定自若地站在他面前，眼对眼瞧着他。

"埃洛伊兹还在那儿，你想想看，我会进你的家门吗？"她说。

⑥ cringe /krɪndʒ/ v. 畏缩，谄媚

哈特利像是被打了一闷棍，软下来了。他两臂交叉放在胸口，又在房间里来回踱了一两趟。

"那就让她走。"他狠下心说，额头上冒出了汗珠。"为什么我要让那女人坏了我的生活？我认识她以后没哪天摆脱过烦恼。维维恩，你说得对，不把埃洛伊兹打发走我不能领你回家。她非走不可。我下了决心。我会把她赶出去的。"

⑦ miserable /'mɪzərəbl/ a. 可悲的，悲惨的

"那你什么时候赶呢？"姑娘问。

哈特利牙一咬，眉一皱。

"今天晚上。"他断然决然说，"今天晚上我就赶她走。"

⑧ clinch /klɪntʃ/ v. 咬紧，捏紧

"那行，我就答应你。"维维恩说，"打发她走了你就来接我。"

她直盯着他的眼睛，表情温柔而恳切。她答应

Hartley could scarcely believe that her surrender was true, it was so swift and complete.

"Promise me," he said feelingly, "on your word and honor."

"On my word and honor," repeated Vivienne, softly.

At the door he turned and gazed at her happily, but yet as one who scarcely trusts the foundations of his joy.

"To-morrow," he said, with a forefinger of reminder uplifted.

"To-morrow," she repeated with a smile of truth and candor.

In an hour and forty minutes Hartley stepped off the train at Floralhurst. A brisk walk of ten minutes brought him to the gate of a handsome two-story cottage set upon a wide and well-tended lawn. Halfway to the house he was met by a woman with jet-black **braided**[①] hair and flowing white summer gown, who half strangled him without apparent cause.

When they stepped into the hall she said:

"Mamma's here. The auto is coming for her in half an hour. She came to dinner, but there's no dinner."

"I've something to tell you," said Hartley. "I thought to break it to you gently, but since your mother is here we may as well out with it."

He stooped and whispered something at her ear.

His wife screamed. Her mother came running into the hall. The dark-haired woman screamed again — the joyful scream of a well-beloved and petted woman.

"Oh, mamma!" she cried **ecstatically**[②], "what do you think? Vivienne is coming to cook for us! She is the one that stayed with the Montgomery's a whole year. And now, Billy, dear," she concluded, "you must go right down into the kitchen and discharge Heloise. She has been drunk again the whole day long."

得太迅速痛快了，哈特利反而不敢信以为真。

"你得言而有信，说话算数。"他深情地说。

"言而有信，说话算数。"维维恩轻轻说。

他走到门边又回过头满心喜悦地注视着他，然而还是担心会空喜一场。

"等着明天！"他说，竖起食指表示叫她别忘了。

"等着明天。"她也说，笑得坦率而真诚。

一小时四十分后哈特利在弗洛勒尔赫斯特下了火车。快步走十分钟，他到了一所漂亮的两层楼小房子的围栏门前，房子坐落在一块修剪得漂亮的大草坪上。进了围栏门还差一半路才到房子时，一个女人不知什么原因一上来几乎将他闷死，这女人穿着宽松的白色夏用长衫，头发乌黑，结成辫子①。

① braid /breɪd/ v. 编辫子

走进门厅后女的说：

"妈妈在家。过半小时汽车来接她。她来吃晚饭，可是没有饭吃。"

哈特利说："我有件重要的事告诉你。原来我想慢慢儿说给你听的，现在你妈妈来了，我们就干脆点儿吧。"

他低下头靠在她耳边轻轻说了句话。

他太太尖声叫起来，他岳母闻声跑进了门厅。黑头发女人又尖声叫起来，是一个被当成心肝宝贝的女人高兴的尖叫。

② ecstatically /ɪkˈstætɪkəlɪ/ a. 狂喜地，心醉神迷地

"哎哟，妈妈，你猜怎么啦？"她喜气洋洋地大声说，"维维恩要来给我们当厨娘！就是在蒙哥马利家干了一年的那一个。比利，亲爱的，你这就到厨房去把埃洛伊兹辞退了。她又喝醉了，一天没省人事。"

奇遇眷顾爱幻想的人。

生活里充满了各种各样的偶然性，如果碰巧我们是有心人，这一个个偶然便定义了我们的人生际遇。

只要你相信，这便是人生的动人之处。

The Green Door

Suppose you should be walking down Broadway after dinner, with ten minutes **allotted**[①] to the **consummation**[②] of your cigar while you are choosing between a diverting tragedy and something serious in the way of **vaudeville**[③]. Suddenly a hand is laid upon your arm. You turn to look into the thrilling eyes of a beautiful woman, wonderful in diamonds and Russian **sables**[④]. She **thrusts**[⑤] hurriedly into your hand an extremely hot buttered roll, flashes out a tiny pair of scissors, **snips**[⑥] off the second button of your overcoat, meaningly **ejaculates**[⑦] the one word, "parallelogram! " and swiftly flies down a cross street, looking back fearfully over her shoulder.

That would be pure adventure. Would you accept it? Not you. You would flush with embarrassment; you would sheepishly drop the roll and continue down Broadway, **fumbling**[⑧] **feebly**[⑨] for the missing button. This you would do unless you are one of the blessed few in whom the pure spirit of adventure is not dead.

True adventurers have never been plentiful. They who are set down in print as such have been mostly business men with newly invented methods. They have been out after the things they wanted — golden

绿色门

你不妨假设此刻你吃过了晚饭，在百老汇路上走，打不定主意该看悲剧消遣，还是到杂艺场看点正经东西，结果一支烟抽了十分钟才抽完。突然有人抓住了你的手。转头一看，原来是个漂亮女人，长着双动人的眼睛，珠光宝气，穿的是俄国黑貂皮衣。她把个热腾腾的奶油圆面包往你手心一塞，亮出把小剪刀，一刀剪下你大衣上的第二颗纽扣，意味深长地说了声"平行四边形"便飞也似的往岔路跑，边跑边惊惶地回头望。

这种事情纯粹是奇遇。你会追那女人吗？不会。你一定是窘得脸发烧，一声不响扔掉圆面包，沿百老汇街继续走，边摸摸第二颗纽扣的扣眼。只有极少数幸运儿单求新奇之心尚未泯灭，如果你不是这种人，一定就是那个样。

一心猎奇的人历来不多。书中所载的冒险家大都为办成一件事，只是方法各异而已。他们的行动有着明确的目的，或为寻金羊毛，或为寻圣杯，或为得女人之爱，或为得财宝，或为得王位，或为得美名。而单纯猎奇的人并无明确目的，机

① allot /əˈlɒt/ v. 分配
② consummation /ˌkɒnsəˈmeɪʃən/ n. 完成，实现
③ vaudeville /ˈvəʊdəvɪl/ n. 轻歌舞剧
④ sable /ˈseɪbl/ n. 貂皮短大衣（或围巾等）
⑤ thrust /θrʌst/ v. 推；刺
⑥ snip /snɪp/ v. 剪
⑦ ejaculate /ɪˈdʒækjʊleɪt/ v. 突然喊出（说出）

⑧ fumble /ˈfʌmbl/ v. 摸索，笨拙地行动
⑨ feebly /ˈfiːblɪ/ ad. 无效地，无益地

fleeces, holy grails, lady loves, treasure, crowns and fame. The true adventurer goes forth aimless and uncalculating to meet and greet unknown fate. A fine example was the Prodigal Son — when he started back home.

Half-adventurers — brave and splendid figures — have been numerous. From the Crusades to the Palisades they have enriched the arts of history and fiction and the trade of historical fiction. But each of them had a prize to win, a goal to kick, an axe to grind, a race to run, a new thrust in **tierce**① to deliver, a name to carve, a crow to pick — so they were not followers of true adventure.

In the big city the twin spirits Romance and Adventure are always abroad seeking worthy wooers. As we roam the streets they **slyly**② peep at us and challenge us in twenty different guises. Without knowing why, we look up suddenly to see in a window a face that seems to belong to our gallery of **intimate**③ **portraits**④; in a sleeping thoroughfare we hear a cry of **agony** ⑤ and fear coming from an empty and shuttered house; instead of at our familiar curb, a cab-driver deposits us before a strange door, which one, with a smile, opens for us and bids us enter; a slip of paper, written upon, flutters down to our feet from the high **lattices**⑥ of Chance; we exchange glances of **instantaneous**⑦ hate, affection and fear with hurrying strangers in the passing crowds; a sudden **douse**⑧ of rain — and our umbrella may be sheltering the daughter of the Full Moon and first cousin of the Sidereal System; at every corner handkerchiefs drop, fingers beckon, eyes **besiege**⑨, and the lost, the lonely, the rapturous, the mysterious, the perilous, changing clues of adventure are slipped into our fingers. But few of us are willing to hold and follow them. We are grown stiff with the **ramrod**⑩ of convention down our backs. We pass on; and some day we come, at the end of a very dull life, to reflect that

缘莫测，以后遇上什么全在未知之列。这种人中
可算为典型的是位浪荡子，他有次回家时的一件
事值得一叙。

不畏险但不求奇的人有勇气，是好汉，古往
今来为数极多，从往日的十字军到今日去帕利塞
德的人都在此列。他们使历史和小说变得丰富多
彩，也给写历史小说这行的人带来了财富。但他
们个个有身手要显，有利益要图，有美名要留，
有怨恨要泄，所以，这些人并不真追求奇遇。

在我们这座大城市里，姻缘与奇遇像两个形
影不离的伙伴，日夜不停地在街上寻找着真正的
有心人。当我们在马路上走时，它们暗暗瞅着我
们，变换各种方式挑逗。例如，偶一抬头时，我
们可能恰在某个窗户里瞥见一张似曾相识的脸；
在一条熟睡了的大街上，我们冷不防听到一所紧
闭着门窗没人住的房子里发出声痛苦而恐惧的尖
叫；马车夫没把我们送到熟悉的人家，却把车停
在一个不认识的人家门口，门一开有人笑脸相迎
请我们进屋；一所不知谁住的高楼上会飘下一张
纸，就落在你跟前，纸上写着字；在来来往往的
人群中，我们与某个陌生人的眼光不期而遇，双
方都流露出憎恨、喜爱或畏惧；天突然落下一阵
雨，与我们共伞的竟是位来历非凡的姑娘或郎君；
随时随地我们都可能遇到人掉手帕，打手势，丢
眼风，这都是奇遇的引线，有无意失落的，有零
星放出的，有高兴时抛下的，神秘莫测，变化多
端，暗藏危机，让我们拾到了。然而我们没几个
人愿意抓住这些引线，沿着引线追踪。陈规像根
棍棒，把我们制服得不能动弹。我们会随手扔掉

① tierce /tɪəs/ *n.* 击剑姿势
（可进行刺杀或闪避）

② slyly /'slaɪlɪ/ *ad.* 狡猾地，
诡诈地

③ intimate /'ɪntɪmɪt/ *a.* 亲密
的，熟悉的

④ portrait /'pɔːtrɪt/ *n.* 肖像，
画像

⑤ agony /'ægənɪ/ *n.* 极度痛
苦，苦恼

⑥ lattice /'lætɪs/ *n.* 格子，格
子窗（或门等）

⑦ instantaneous
/ɪnstən'teɪnɪəs/ *a.* 瞬间的，
实时的

⑧ douse /daʊs/ *n.* 水泼

⑨ besiege /bɪ'siːdʒ/ *v.* 围困，
包围

⑩ ramrod /'ræm‚rɒd/ *n.* 通
条

our romance has been a **pallid**① thing of a marriage or two, a **satin**②
rosette③ kept in a safe-deposit drawer, and a lifelong feud with a steam
radiator.

Rudolf Steiner was a true adventurer. Few were the evenings on
which he did not go forth from his hall **bedchamber**④ in search of the
unexpected and the **egregious**⑤. The most interesting thing in life seemed
to him to be what might lie just around the next corner. Sometimes his
willingness to tempt fate led him into strange paths. Twice he had spent
the night in a station-house; again and again he had found himself the
dupe of ingenious and mercenary tricksters; his watch and money had
been the price of one flattering **allurement**⑥. But with undiminished
ardor⑦ he picked up every glove cast before him into the merry lists of
adventure.

One evening Rudolf was strolling along a crosstown street in the
older central part of the city. Two streams of people filled the sidewalks
— the home-hurrying, and that restless **contingent**⑧ that abandons home
for the specious welcome of the thousand-candle-power "table d'hote".

The young adventurer was of pleasing presence, and moved
serenely and watchfully. By daylight he was a salesman in a piano store.
He wore his tie drawn through a **topaz**⑨ ring instead of fastened with a
stick pin; and once he had written to the editor of a magazine that
"Junie's Love Test" by Miss Libbey, had been the book that had most
influenced his life.

During his walk a violent chattering of teeth in a glass case on the
sidewalk seemed at first to draw his attention (with a qualm), to a
restaurant before which it was set; but a second glance **revealed**⑩ the
electric letters of a dentist's sign high above the next door. A giant
negro, fantastically dressed in a red **embroidered**⑪ coat, yellow trousers

① pallid /'pælɪd/ a. 苍白的,
没血色的

② satin /'sætɪn/ a. 似缎的,光
滑柔软的

③ rosette /rəʊ'zet/ n. 玫瑰花
形物

④ bedchamber
/'bed,tʃeɪmbə/ n. 卧室

⑤ egregious /ɪ'griːdʒəs/ a.
极坏的,极糟的

⑥ allurement /ə'ljʊəmənt/ n.
诱惑

⑦ ardor /'ɑːdə/ n. 热心

⑧ contingent /kən'tɪndʒənt/
n. 分遣队,组

⑨ topaz /'təʊpæz/ n. 黄玉

⑩ reveal /rɪ'viːl/ v. 揭露,展
现

⑪ embroider /ɪm'brɔɪdə/ v. 刺
绣,渲染

这些引线。等到有一天一辈子的枯燥生活要完结了,我们才会醒悟,发觉我们的情场经历无声无色,不过是结一两次婚,或者是用保险柜收藏个丝绸蝴蝶结,或者是跟一个火爆脾气闹一生别扭。

鲁道夫·斯坦纳是个真心追求奇遇的人。他几乎天天夜里要从他住的公寓出来,想遇到些意料不到的稀奇事。在他看来,生活中最有意味的事只要你再走过一个街口就会发生。有时候碰运气的心理使他走上了迷途。他曾在车站待过两夜,被狡诈的骗子骗过好些回,有次让人灌了花言巧语的迷魂汤,损失了手表和钱。但他依然兴致勃勃,抓住一切机会追求奇遇。

一天晚上,鲁道夫在老市中心沿着一条穿城马路闲逛。两旁人行道上行人如潮,有的脚步匆匆往家里赶,也有的在家里闷得慌,便来到灯火通明的餐馆点上一桌华而不实的"套餐"。

这位兴致勃勃的年轻人衣冠楚楚,悠闲地走路,眼睛四下里瞧。白天他在一家钢琴店站柜台。他的领带上装饰的不是根别针,而是黄晶圈。有一次他写信给一家杂志的编辑说,利比小姐写的《朱尼的爱情考验》是对他的生活最有影响的书。

走着走着,他听到人行道旁有牙齿发颤的响声,觉得奇怪,一看,原来是摆在一家餐馆前的玻璃盒里的牙齿发出的,再瞧瞧又发现餐馆边房子的楼上高挂着牙科诊所的霓虹灯招牌。一个大

and a **military**① cap, **discreetly**② distributed cards to those of the passing crowd who consented to take them.

This mode of dentistic advertising was a common sight to Rudolf. Usually he passed the **dispenser**③ of the dentist's cards without reducing his store; but tonight the African slipped one into his hand so deftly that he retained it there smiling a little at the successful feat.

When he had travelled a few yards further he glanced at the card indifferently. Surprised, he turned it over and looked again with interest. One side of the card was blank; on the other was written in ink three words, "The Green Door." And then Rudolf saw, three steps in front of him, a man throw down the card the negro had given him as he passed. Rudolf picked it up. It was printed with the dentist's name and address and the usual schedule of "plate work" and "bridge work" and specious promises of "painless" operations.

The adventurous piano salesman halted at the corner and considered. Then he crossed the street, walked down a block, recrossed and joined the upward current of people again. Without seeming to notice the negro as he passed the second time, he carelessly took the card that was handed him. Ten steps away he inspected it. In the same handwriting that appeared on the first card "The Green Door" was inscribed upon it. Three or four cards were **tossed**④ to the pavement by pedestrians both following and leading him. These fell blank side up. Rudolf turned them over. Every one bore the printed legend of the dental "parlors."

Rarely did the arch sprite Adventure need to **beckon**⑤ twice to Rudolf Steiner, his true follower. But twice it had been done, and the quest was on.

Rudolf walked slowly back to where the giant negro stood by the

个子黑人穿得怪里怪气，上身是红绣花衣，下身是黄裤子，头戴军帽，见到行人有愿接他的名片的，他才送上一张。

牙科医生做广告的这种方式鲁道夫已司空见惯。往常他从这种散发牙科医生名片的人身边经过时不接名片，但这天晚上例外，黑人手巧，竟塞给了他一张，他非但未拒绝，而且一笑，佩服他的高招。

往前走了几步后他瞟了一眼名片。竟有他没想到的事，觉得有趣，把名片翻过来再看看。原来名片的一面是空白，另一面写着三个字：绿色门。再一抬头，只见前面三步外的一个人把黑人给他的名片扔了。鲁道夫捡了起来。上面印的是牙科医生的姓名和住址，还有"补牙""架桥""镶牙"时间表及吹嘘手术"无痛"等大话。

热心奇遇的钢琴店售货员站在十字路口旁想了一会儿。然后他横过马路，走过一个路口，再横过马路，混进了人流中往回走。再从那黑人身边过时，他故意没有瞟那黑人，只顺手接过递给他的名片。走出十步他一看，见上面仍写着"绿色门"，笔迹与第一张名片上的完全相同。地上还有他前前后后的行人扔掉的三四张，空白面朝上。鲁道夫把它们翻过来，发现都印着牙科诊所自吹自擂的话。

鲁道夫·斯坦纳本是个一心求奇遇的人，难得使奇遇之神向他招两次手。现在已经招了两次手，他于是就开始追寻。

鲁道夫掉转身慢慢向大个子黑人走去，那黑

case of **rattling**[1] teeth. This time as he passed he received no card. In spite of his **gaudy**[2] and ridiculous garb, the Ethiopian displayed a natural **barbaric**[3] dignity as he stood, offering the cards **suavely**[4] to some, allowing others to pass **unmolested**[5]. Every half minute he chanted a harsh, unintelligible phrase akin to the jabber of car conductors and grand opera. And not only did he withhold a card this time, but it seemed to Rudolf that he received from the shining and massive black **countenance**[6] a look of cold, almost **contemptuous**[7] **disdain**[8].

The look stung the adventurer. He read in it a silent **accusation**[9] that he had been found wanting. Whatever the mysterious written words on the cards might mean, the black had selected him twice from the throng for their recipient; and now seemed to have condemned him as deficient in the wit and spirit to engage the enigma.

Standing aside from the rush, the young man made a rapid estimate of the building in which he conceived that his adventure must lie. Five stories high it rose. A small restaurant occupied the basement.

The first floor, now closed, seemed to house millinery or furs. The second floor, by the winking electric letters, was the dentist's. Above this a polyglot babel of signs struggled to indicate the **abodes**[10] of palmists, dressmakers, musicians and doctors. Still higher up draped curtains and milk bottles white on the window sills proclaimed the regions of domesticity.

After concluding his survey Rudolf walked briskly up the high flight of stone steps into the house. Up two flights of the carpeted stairway he continued; and at its top paused. The hallway there was dimly lighted by two pale jets of gas one — far to his right, the other nearer, to his left. He looked toward the nearer light and saw, within its wan halo, a green door.

① rattling /'rætlɪŋ/ a. 格格作响的

② gaudy /'gɔːdɪ/ a.（文风、服饰等）华丽而俗气的

③ barbaric /bɑː'bærɪk/ a. 野蛮的,残暴的

④ suavely /'sweɪvlɪ/ ad. 温文尔雅地,讨好地

⑤ unmolested /'ʌnmə'lestɪd/ a. 不受烦扰的,不受干扰的

⑥ countenance /'kaʊntɪnəns/ n. 脸部表情

⑦ contemptuous /kən'temptjʊəs/ a. 表示轻蔑的;藐视的

⑧ disdain /dɪ'sdeɪn/ n. 蔑视

⑨ accusation /ˌækjʊ'zeɪʃən/ n. 指责

⑩ abode /ə'bəʊd/ n. 住所,住处

人仍站在装着咯咯发响的牙齿的玻璃盒边。这次他从他身边过时没接到名片。尽管黑人的穿着花哨古怪,神态却是粗犷中有庄重,遇上愿接名片的人他会彬彬有礼送上一张,遇上不愿接的并不强求。每隔半分钟他会像车上的售票员那样,也像在演大歌剧那样,拉开粗嗓门吆喝一声,吆喝的什么也听不清。这次他不但没有给名片,而且鲁道夫觉得他那黑得发亮的大脸现出了冷淡的、近似鄙夷的表情。

这表情让追求奇遇的人见了不大好受。他认为尽管没有说,那黑人只当自己高抬了他。无论那张神秘的纸片上写的几个字是什么意思,反正黑人两次都只当他与众不同,值得送。现在黑人似乎是怪他既不聪明,又少勇气,不配解开这个谜。

年轻人站到人流外,把他认为一定会有奇遇的这座房子上上下下看了一眼。房子共五层,底层是家小餐馆。

二楼关着,似乎堆放着帽子和毛皮衣。三楼的霓虹灯招牌一亮一灭,是牙科医生的诊所。往上的招牌五花八门,有手相师的,有裁缝店的,乐队的,诊所的。再往上的窗户挂着窗帘,窗台上放着白牛奶瓶,显然是住房。

鲁道夫打量一番后快步走上高高的石头台阶进了屋子。他一口气爬了两层铺了地毯的楼梯,在楼梯口站住了。走廊上光线暗淡,点着两盏小气灯,一盏在他右边,离得远,一盏在左边,离得近些。他朝离他近的一头望去,看见昏暗的灯下有一扇绿色的门。犹豫了一会儿后,他仿佛看

For one moment he hesitated; then he seemed to see the **contumelious**[1] sneer of the African juggler of cards; and then he walked straight to the green door and knocked against it.

Moments like those that passed before his knock was answered measure the quick breath of true adventure. What might not be behind those green panels! Gamesters at play; cunning **rogues**[2] baiting their traps with subtle skill; beauty in love with courage, and thus planning to be sought by it; danger, death, love, disappointment, **ridicule**[3] — any of these might respond to that **temerarious**[4] rap.

A faint rustle was heard inside, and the door slowly opened. A girl not yet twenty stood there, white-faced and tottering. She loosed the knob and **swayed**[5] weakly, groping with one hand. Rudolf caught her and laid her on a faded couch that stood against the wall. He closed the door and took a swift glance around the room by the light of a flickering gas jet. Neat, but extreme poverty was the story that he read.

The girl lay still, as if in a faint. Rudolf looked around the room excitedly for a barrel. People must be rolled upon a barrel who — no, no; that was for drowned persons. He began to fan her with his hat. That was successful, for he struck her nose with the **brim**[6] of his **derby**[7] and she opened her eyes. And then the young man saw that hers, indeed, was the one missing face from his heart's gallery of intimate portraits. The frank, grey eyes, the little nose, turning pertly outward; the **chestnut**[8] hair, curling like the tendrils of a pea vine, seemed the right end and reward of all his wonderful adventures. But the face was woefully thin and pale.

The girl looked at him calmly, and then smiled.

"Fainted, didn't I? " she asked, weakly. "Well, who wouldn't? You try going without anything to eat for three days and see! "

① contumelious
/ˌkɒntjuːˈmiːlɪəs/ a. 无礼的,傲慢的

② rogue /rəʊg/ n. 恶棍,调皮鬼

③ ridicule /ˈrɪdɪkjuːl/ n. 嘲笑,揶揄

④ temerarious
/ˌteməˈreərɪəs/ a. 不顾一切的,鲁莽的

⑤ sway /sweɪ/ v. 摇动,摇摆

⑥ brim /brɪm/ n.（容器）边,缘

⑦ derby /ˈdɑːbɪ/ n. 圆顶窄边礼帽

⑧ chestnut /ˈtʃesˌnʌt/ n. 栗子

到了那拿名片变戏法的黑人鄙夷的目光,便直朝那扇绿门走去,敲了敲。

他敲过以后好大一会儿里面才有声响,可见当真会有奇遇。各种各样的事都出在这种绿色门后!有聚赌的,有滑头鬼设下巧计勾人上当的,有美人儿胆大幽会的,因此到了这种地方,冒冒失失一敲门各种可能性都会出现,或遇险,或出人命,或得爱情,或大失所望,或受到奚落。

房间里隐隐有衣裙的窸窣声,接着门慢慢开了。门里站着位姑娘,不到二十岁,脸无血色,脚发软。她放开了门把手后,身子有气无力地晃起来,伸出一只手想抓住什么。鲁道夫赶忙抱起她,放到靠墙的一张掉了色的卧榻上。他关上门,借着闪闪烁烁的煤气灯把房间四下里看了一眼。干净倒是干净,但主人穷到了极点。

姑娘躺着一动不动,像是昏了过去。鲁道夫急了,眼到处望,想找个圆桶。昏过去的人得放在圆桶上滚。但再一想又不对,是溺水昏过去的才用圆桶滚。他取下帽子给她扇着。这一招收了效,因为帽边碰着了她的鼻子,她睁开了眼睛。年轻人这才发现,姑娘的脸是他的心久久向往的脸。灰眼睛里的眼神坦率,小鼻子俏皮地稍稍往上翘,棕色头发鬈曲着,像豌豆藤上的小须。他追求奇遇的目的就在这里,这一次看来不虚此行。可惜的是,这张脸又瘦又惨白。

姑娘定睛看着他,然后一笑。

"我昏过去了,是吗?"她用微弱的声音问道,"哎,有谁能不昏过去?叫你也三天什么都不吃,你试试看!"

"Himmel!" exclaimed Rudolf, jumping up. "Wait till I come back."

He dashed out the green door and down the stairs. In twenty minutes he was back again, kicking at the door with his toe for her to open it. With both arms he hugged an **array**① of wares from the grocery and the restaurant. On the table he laid them — bread and butter, cold meats, cakes, pies, pickles, oysters, a roasted chicken, a bottle of milk and one of redhot tea.

"This is ridiculous," said Rudolf, blusteringly, "to go without eating. You must quit making election bets of this kind. Supper is ready." He helped her to a chair at the table and asked: "Is there a cup for the tea? " "On the shelf by the window," she answered. When he turned again with the cup he saw her, with eyes shining **rapturously** ②, beginning upon a huge Dill pickle that she had rooted out from the paper bags with a woman's **unerring** ③ instinct. He took it from her, laughingly, and poured the cup full of milk. "Drink that first" he ordered, "and then you shall have some tea, and then a chicken wing. If you are very good you shall have a pickle to-morrow. And now, if you'll allow me to be your guest we'll have supper."

He drew up the other chair. The tea brightened the girl's eyes and brought back some of her color. She began to eat with a sort of dainty **ferocity**④ like some starved wild animal. She seemed to regard the young man's presence and the aid he had rendered her as a natural thing — not as though she **undervalued** ⑤ the conventions; but as one whose great stress gave her the right to put aside the artificial for the human. But gradually, with the return of strength and comfort, came also a sense of the little conventions that belong; and she began to tell him her little story. It was one of a thousand such as the city yawns at every day — the shop girl's story of insufficient wages, further reduced by "fines" that

"我的妈呀！"鲁道夫说着一跃而起，"你等等，我马上就来。"

他冲出绿色门，跑下楼梯。二十分钟后，他赶回来了，用脚尖踢着门，叫她开。他双手抱着一大堆吃的，有杂货店买的，也有餐馆买的，往桌上一放，是奶油面包、各色冷肉、蛋糕、馅饼、腌黄瓜、牡蛎、一只烤鸡、一瓶牛奶，一瓶滚烫的茶。

"真是荒唐，人还能够不吃饭？"鲁道夫大声说，"这种事以后千万别再干！现在吃饭吧。"他把她扶到桌边坐下，问道，"有杯子倒茶吗？"姑娘答道："窗口边的架上有。"等他拿了茶杯再转身时，只见她高兴得眼闪闪发亮，已开始吃起来，而且凭着女人心细的天性，挑的是纸袋里一条大腌黄瓜。他笑着抢走她手里的黄瓜，倒了满满一杯牛奶，嘱咐道："先喝牛奶，再喝茶，然后吃只鸡翅膀。等到恢复了元气，明天才可以吃腌黄瓜。我做你的客人，我们一道吃，行吗？"

他端来另一把椅子。喝过茶，姑娘开始有了血色，眼也变明亮了。她狼吞虎咽般大口吃起来。桌边还坐了个年轻人她满不在乎，吃的东西是人家买来的她只当没关系，这倒不是因为没把陈规放在眼里，而是因为饿得慌，理所当然要抛开人为的客套。但是等到渐渐地体力恢复，有了精神后，她也感到该讲点应有的礼节，向他说出了自己究竟出了什么事。原来，这种事每天发生上千起，纽约人已习以为常。她原在商店当售货员，工资微薄，还受到"罚款"（是进商店老板腰包

① array /əˈreɪ/ n. （排列整齐的）一批

② rapturously /ˈræptʃərəslɪ/ ad. 兴高采烈地

③ unerring /ˈʌnˈɜːrɪŋ/ a. 没错的，准确的

④ ferocity /fəˈrɒsɪtɪ/ n. 凶猛，残暴

⑤ undervalue /ˌʌndəˈvæljuː/ v. 低估价值，看轻

go to swell the store's profits; of time lost through illness; and then of lost positions, lost hope, and — the knock of the adventurer upon the green door.

But to Rudolf the history sounded as big as the Iliad or the crisis in "Junie's Love Test."

"To think of you going through all that," he exclaimed.

"It was something fierce," said the girl, solemnly.

"And you have no relatives or friends in the city? "

"None whatever."

"I am all alone in the world, too," said Rudolf, after a pause.

"I am glad of that," said the girl, promptly; and somehow it pleased the young man to hear that she approved of his **bereft** ① condition.

Very suddenly her eyelids dropped and she sighed deeply.

"I'm awfully sleepy," she said, "and I feel so good."

Then Rudolf rose and took his hat. "I'll say good-night. A long night's sleep will be fine for you."

He held out his hand, and she took it and said "good-night." But her eyes asked a question so **eloquently**②, so frankly and **pathetically**③ that he answered it with words.

"Oh, I'm coming back to-morrow to see how you are getting along. You can't get rid of me so easily."

Then, at the door, as though the way of his coming had been so much less important than the fact that he had come, she asked: "How did you come to knock at my door? "

He looked at her for a moment, remembering the cards, and felt a sudden jealous pain. What if they had fallen into other hands as adventurous as his? Quickly he decided that she must never know the

的罚款），后来又生病上不了班，接着丢了饭碗，陷入绝境，却没料这位追求奇遇的人来敲她的绿色门。

但在鲁道夫听来，她说的经历就像诗《伊利亚特》和小说《朱尼的爱情考验》一样震撼。

"没想到你会受这种磨难。"他说。

"说起来是够凄惨了。"姑娘的语气沉重。

"你在纽约没有亲戚或者朋友吗?"

"一个也没有。"

鲁道夫没马上接话，过了会儿才说："我在这世上也是孤身一人。"

"我看这样更好。"姑娘的话来得唐突，但年轻人一听她竟然巴不得他孤身一人，内心很有几分高兴。

突然她撑不开眼皮，深深叹口气，说："我很想睡了，现在我感觉好多了。"

鲁道夫起身拿好帽子。

"那我就告辞了。夜晚睡上一大觉对你有好处。"

他伸出只手，姑娘握着手说了声"再见"。但是看眼神她还有所求，内心的思想表露得那么明显、坦率、叫人感动，年轻人用言语作了回答。

"好，我明天再来看看你身体恢复得怎样。短时间你还少不了我。"

她似乎就关心他是怎样来的，倒忘了他来救了她，走到门边时问道："你怎么会敲我的门呢?"

他看了她好一会儿，想起那两张纸片，心头突然觉得又酸又难受。如果它们落到了另一个与

① bereft /bɪˈreft/ a. 丧失了亲人的,孤寂的,凄凉的

② eloquently /ˈeləkwəntlɪ/ ad. 善辩地,富于表现力地

③ pathetically /pəˈθetɪkəlɪ/ ad. 可怜地,可悲地

truth. He would never let her know that he was aware of the strange expedient to which she had been driven by her great **distress**①.

"One of our piano tuners lives in this house," he said. "I knocked at your door by mistake."

The last thing he saw in the room before the green door closed was her smile.

At the head of the stairway he paused and looked curiously about him. And then he went along the hallway to its other end; and, coming back, **ascended** ② to the floor above and continued his puzzled explorations. Every door that he found in the house was painted green.

Wondering, he descended to the sidewalk. The fantastic African was still there. Rudolf **confronted**③ him with his two cards in his hand.

"Will you tell me why you gave me these cards and what they mean? " he asked.

In a broad, good-natured grin the negro exhibited a splendid advertisement of his master's profession.

"Dar it is, boss," he said, pointing down the street. "But I 'spect you is a little late for de fust act."

Looking the way he pointed Rudolf saw above the entrance to a theatre the **blazing**④ electric sign of its new play, "The Green Door."

"I'm informed dat it's a fust-rate show, sah," said the negro. "De agent what represents it pussented me with a dollar, sah, to distribute a few of his cards along with de doctah's. May I offer you one of de doctah's cards, sah? "

At the corner of the block in which he lived Rudolf stopped for a glass of beer and a cigar. When he had come out with his lighted weed he buttoned his coat, pushed back his hat and said, stoutly, to the lamp post on the corner:

① distress /dɪ'stres/ n. 悲痛,
苦恼

他同样追求奇遇的人手中,结果会如何呢?他当即打定主意,不把事实真相告诉她。决不能让她知道他心中完全有数,她是出于痛苦的生活所迫,才采用了这种少有的权宜之计。

"我们店有位调琴师住在这房子里,我是错敲了你的门。"他说。

绿色门关上了,房间里什么他都没看见,只看见她的一丝微笑。

② ascend /ə'send/ v. 登高,
上升

走到楼梯口他站住了,出于好奇心看了看四周。然后他沿走廊走到尽头,再折回来,爬上另外一层,要看个究竟。他发现这所房子每扇门都是漆成绿色。

③ confront /kən'frʌnt/ v. 遭
遇

他迷惑不解,下了楼,回到人行道上。那穿得怪里怪气的黑人还在。鲁道夫拿着两张纸片走到他面前。

"请问,你为什么给我这两张纸片,它们是怎么回事?"

黑人态度亲切,咧开大嘴笑着,露出的那口白牙可说是他老板手艺的活招牌。

④ blazing /'bleɪzɪŋ/ a. 燃烧
的,炽烈的

他往前面一指,说:"先生请看那儿,不过恐怕第一幕你已赶不上了。"

鲁道夫顺他指的方向看去,见到一家剧院大门的霓虹灯亮着新上演剧目的剧名:绿色门。

黑人说:"先生,我听说这剧好看得很呐。剧院的人给了我一块钱,叫我在散发医生的名片时也帮他散发几张。医生的名片你要不要?"

回到他住处近旁的街口,鲁道夫喝了杯啤酒,点了根烟。出店门后烟还没抽完,他扣上衣服,往后挪挪帽子,对着街口的灯柱毫不犹豫地说:

"All the same, I believe it was the hand of Fate that doped out the way for me to find her."

Which conclusion, under the circumstances, certainly admits Rudolf Steiner to the ranks of the true followers of Romance and Adventure.

"反正是一回事。我相信我见到她是命里注定。"

有人因追寻奇遇而得姻缘，现在这件事的结局说明，鲁道夫·斯坦纳便是这么一个人。

这是一个逗趣的故事。

人们的心情和行为如何受到四时左右，可真是有趣的事。"在五月，大自然伸出指头指着我们的鼻子，叫我们别忘了我们不是神，只是她的大家庭的成员。"

春天万物生发，人们也顺应其时，开始不安分起来，且看五月这个捣蛋小精灵如何搞它的恶作剧吧。

The Marry Month of May

Prithee, smite the poet in the eye when he would sing to you praises of the month of May. It is a month presided over by the spirits of mischief and madness. Pixies and **flibbertigibbets** [1] haunt the budding woods: Puck and his train of midgets are busy in town and country.

In May nature holds up at us a chiding finger, bidding us remember that we are not gods, but overconceited members of her own great family. She reminds us that we are brothers to the chowder-doomed clam and the donkey; lineal scions of the pansy and the chimpanzee, and but cousins-german to the cooing doves, the quacking ducks and the housemaids and policemen in the parks.

In May Cupid shoots **blindfolded** [2] — millionaires marry stenographers; wise professors woo white-aproned gum-chewers behind quick-lunch counters; schoolma'ams make big bad boys remain after school; lads with ladders steal lightly over lawns where Juliet waits in her **trellissed** [3] window with her telescope packed; young couples out for a walk come home married; old chaps put on white spats and promenade near the Normal School; even married men, grown **unwontedly** [4] tender and **sentimental** [5], whack their spouses on the back and growl: "How

五月是个结婚月

① flibbertigibbet
/'flɪbətɪ'dʒɪbɪt/ *n.* 饶舌的
人，轻浮的人

② blindfold /'blaɪndfəʊld/ *v.*
蒙住（眼睛）

③ trellis /'trelɪs/ *v.* 为……
搭棚架

④ unwonted /ʌn'wəʊntɪd/ *a.*
不习惯的，不寻常的

⑤ sentimental /ˌsentɪ'mentl/
a. 情深的，多情的；感情
用事的

如果诗人在君前歌颂五月，请君当头给他狠狠一棒。五月是捣蛋乱来的小精灵得意忘形的时候。那帮淘气包不仅仅出没于刚发芽返青的树林里，他们的恶作剧简直肆虐城乡。

五月，大自然伸出个指头指着我们的鼻子，叫我们别忘了我们不是神，而只是她的大家庭的成员，不过自以为了不起罢了。大自然还提醒我们，我们与当作盘中餐的蚌与驴是亲兄弟；是黑猩猩的直系子孙；咕咕咕的鸽子也好，嘎嘎嘎的鸭子也好，我们自己也好，女佣和公园的警察也好，都是堂亲和表亲。

五月，丘比特蒙着眼睛乱射箭，结果百万富翁娶了速记员；头脑里装满智慧的教授在快餐柜台后向系白围裙、嚼口香糖的女人求爱；放学后，女老师把大个子坏学生留在学校；小伙子搬着梯子偷偷溜到草地上，姑娘早拿着望远镜趴在格子窗上等着；一对年轻人出门散次步回家便结了婚；老家伙穿着白鞋罩在师范学校附近闲逛；甚至结婚多年的人都变得柔情脉脉，拍着老伴的背粗声粗气地问：

goes it, old girl? "

This May, who is no goddess, but Circe, masquerading at the dance given in honor of the fair **debutante**①, Summer, **puts the kibosh on**② us all.

Old Mr. Coulson **groaned**③ a little, and then sat up straight in his **invalid**④'s chair. He had the **gout**⑤ very bad in one foot, a house near Gramercy Park, half a million dollars and a daughter. And he had a housekeeper, Mrs. Widdup. The fact and the name deserve a sentence each. They have it.

When May poked Mr. Coulson he became elder brother to the turtle-dove. In the window near which he sat were boxes of **jonquils**⑥, of **hyacinths**⑦, **geraniums**⑧ and pansies. The breeze brought their odor into the room. Immediately there was a well-contested round between the breath of the flowers and the able and active **effluvium**⑨ from gout **liniment**⑩. The liniment won easily; but not before the flowers got an uppercut to old Mr. Coulson's nose. The deadly work of the implacable, false **enchantress**⑪ May was done.

Across the park to the olfactories of Mr. Coulson came other unmistakable, characteristic, copyrighted smells of spring that belong to the-big-city-above-the-Subway, alone. The smells of hot **asphalt**⑫, underground caverns, gasoline, patchouli, orange peel, sewer gas, Albany grabs, Egyptian cigarettes, **mortar**⑬ and the undried ink on newspapers. The inblowing air was sweet and mild. Sparrows **wrangled**⑭ happily everywhere outdoors. Never trust May.

Mr. Coulson twisted the ends of his white mustache, cursed his foot, and pounded a bell on the table by his side.

In came Mrs. Widdup. She was comely to the eye, fair, **flustered**⑮, forty and foxy.

"那事怎么样，亲爱的？"

今年的五月也是妖不是神，就在夏日刚来之际，发生了一件叫我们大家都意想不到的事。

库尔森老先生躺在椅上呻吟了好一阵才坐起身。他的一只脚风湿痛发得厉害，他在格勒默西公园近旁有栋房子，存款五十万美元，还有个女儿。他请了个女管家，叫威达普太太。这件事与女管家的姓氏值得交代一笔，我便交代了一笔。

到了五月，库尔森先生便快活得像只斑鸠。他坐在窗子近边，窗台上摆着长寿花、风信子、天竺葵、三色紫罗兰。微风把它们的清香吹进房里。花儿的清香一进房，立刻与痛风膏发出的强烈气味展开了搏斗。药膏轻易取胜，但只是在花香飘过库尔森老先生身边后才谈得上轻易。五月这难对付、爱乱来的妖孽的勾当不会白干。

库尔森先生的嗅觉也闻到了公园对过有地铁的大城市才有的春天的气息，它们的味道分明、独特，不可复制，有发热的柏油味，地下的大窟窿味，汽油味，薄荷香水味，橘皮味，水沟臭味，阿尔巴尼海蚌味，埃及烟味，灰泥味，还有报纸未干的油墨味。吹进房里的空气甜美柔和。房子外到处有麻雀在快乐地叽叽喳喳。但你绝不要轻信五月。

库尔森先生捏着往两边翘的白胡须，又埋怨自己的脚，埋怨过后便使劲一敲身边桌子上的铃。

威达普太太闻声走了进来。她这人中看，皮肤白，进来时神色紧张。她四十岁，是个滑头。

"希金斯出去了，老爷。"她笑着说，笑里藏

① debutante /ˌdebjuˈtɑːnt/ n. 初次进入社交界的女子

② put the kibosh on （俚）结束，压制，阻止

③ groan /grəʊn/ v. 呻吟，叹息

④ invalid /ˈɪnvəlɪd/ n. 病弱的人

⑤ gout /gaʊt/ n. [医] 痛风

⑥ jonquil /ˈdʒɒŋkwɪl/ n. 长寿花，黄水仙

⑦ hyacinth /ˈhaɪəsɪnθ/ n. 风信子，百合科植物

⑧ geranium /dʒɪˈreɪnjəm/ n. 天竺葵

⑨ effluvium /eˈfluːvɪəm/ n. 臭气

⑩ liniment /ˈlɪnɪmənt/ n. 擦剂，搽剂

⑪ enchantress /ɪnˈtʃɑːntrɪs/ n. 女巫，妖妇

⑫ asphalt /ˈæsfælt/ n. 沥青，柏油

⑬ mortar /ˈmɔːtə/ n. 灰浆

⑭ wrangle /ˈræŋgl/ v. 争吵，争辩

⑮ fluster /ˈflʌstə(r)/ v. 使慌张；使激动

"Higgins is out, sir," she said, with a smile suggestive of **vibratory**[1] massage. "He went to post a letter. Can I do anything for you, sir? "

"It's time for my aconite," said old Mr. Coulson. "Drop it for me. The bottle's there. Three drops. In water. D — that is, confound Higgins! There's nobody in this house cares if I die here in this chair for want of attention."

Mrs. Widdup sighed deeply.

"Don't be saying that, sir," she said. "There's them that would care more than any one knows. Thirteen drops, you said, sir? "

"Three," said old man Coulson.

He took his dose and then Mrs. Widdup's hand. She blushed. Oh, yes, it can be done. Just hold your breath and compress the **diaphragm**[2].

"Mrs. Widdup," said Mr. Coulson, "the springtime's full upon us."

"Ain't that right? " said Mrs. Widdup. "The air's real warm. And there's bock-beer signs on every corner. And the park's all yaller and pink and blue with flowers; and I have such shooting pains up my legs and body."

"'In the spring,'" quoted Mr. Coulson, curling his mustache, "'ay — that is, a man's — fancy lightly turns to thoughts of love.'"

"Lawsy, now! " exclaimed Mrs. Widdup; "ain't that right? Seems like it's in the air."

"'In the spring,'" continued old Mr. Coulson, "'a livelier iris shines upon the burnished dove.'"

"They do be lively, the Irish," sighed Mrs. Widdup pensively.

"Mrs. Widdup," said Mr. Coulson, making a face at a twinge of his gouty foot, "this would be a lonesome house without you. I'm an — that

① vibratory /ˈvaɪbrətərɪ/ *a.*
振动的，颤动的

着撩人的深意，"他出去寄信。老爷有什么吩咐？"

"我该吃附子啦，"库尔森老先生说，"你给我倒。瓶子在那儿。三滴。要兑水。医……就他妈的希金斯混蛋！我没个人侍候，就是死在椅上家里也不会有哪个在乎。"

威达普太太使劲叹口气。

"老爷别说得这个样，只怕是在乎了还没人知道哟！老爷，你是说十三滴吧？"她问。

"三滴！"库尔森老头说。

他吃完药抓着威达普太太的手。威达普太太脸红了。要脸红并不难，只要屏住气息，压迫横膈膜就行。

② diaphragm /ˈdaɪəfræm/ *n.*
膜片，隔膜

"威达普太太，春已深了。"库尔森先生说。

"那还不好吗？"威达普太太说，"天气已经转暖，哪个角落里的气象都不同了。公园里开了黄花、红花、蓝花，我发了腿痛，一身痛。"

库尔森先生把两撇胡须一翘，感叹说："到了春天——哎，到春天人就——人就有点儿想着爱情。"

"看你说的！"威达普太太大声道，"想到又怎么着？现在爱情用鼻子都闻得着哩。"

库尔森老先生继续扯了下去："到了春天，油亮的鸽子更叫人爱。"

"油里的鸽子是叫人爱吃。"威达普太太感慨地叹了口气。

库尔森先生害风湿痛的脚一抽搐，痛得他做了个怪相，但他还是说："威达普太太，这屋子

is, I'm an elderly man — but I'm worth a comfortable lot of money. If half a million dollars' worth of Government bonds and the true affection of a heart that, though no longer beating with the first ardor of youth, can still throb with genuine — "

The loud noise of an overturned chair near the portieres of the **adjoining** ① room interrupted the **venerable** ② and scarcely suspecting victim of May.

In stalked Miss Van Meeker Constantia Coulson, bony, durable, tall, high-nosed, frigid, well-bred, thirty-five, in-the-neighbourhood-of-Gramercy-Parkish. She put up a **lorgnette**③. Mrs. Widdup hastily stooped and arranged the bandages on Mr. Coulson's gouty foot.

"I thought Higgins was with you," said Miss Van Meeker Constantia.

"Higgins went out," explained her father, "and Mrs. Widdup answered the bell. That is better now, Mrs. Widdup, thank you. No, there is nothing else I require."

The housekeeper retired, pink under the cool, inquiring stare of Miss Coulson.

"This spring weather is lovely, isn't it, daughter? " said the old man, consciously conscious.

"That's just it," replied Miss Van Meeker Constantia Coulson, somewhat **obscurely**④. "When does Mrs. Widdup start on her vacation, papa? "

"I believe she said a week from to-day," said Mr. Coulson.

Miss Van Meeker Constantia stood for a minute at the window gazing, toward the little park, flooded with the mellow afternoon sunlight. With the eye of a botanist she viewed the flowers — most

没有了你会变得冷清清。我已经——已经是上了年纪的人。可是呢，我那一大堆票子还不会白白搁着。要是价值五十万美元的公债还顶用，要是一颗真有感情的心——就算这颗心不像年轻人的热得像火——要是它跳起来还真……"

摆在隔壁房间门边的一张椅子倒了地，咣当一声，打断了这位中了五月的邪气的老先生的话。

范·米克·康斯坦霞·库尔森小姐昂首阔步闯了进来。她瘦而精神，个子高，鼻子也高，不动感情，教养倒好，年已三十五岁，也是守着格勒默西公园长大的人。她举起长柄眼镜一瞧。威达普太太赶紧弯下身给库尔森先生发风湿痛的脚扎绷带。

"我还以为希金斯在你这儿。"范·米克·康斯坦霞小姐说。

"希金斯出去了，威达普太太听到铃响来了。"她父亲解释道，"现在痛得好些了。谢谢你，威达普太太。行啦，我现在没别的事了。"

管家走了出去，脸发烧，是让库尔森小姐冷冰冰的怀疑目光看得发烧的。

"今年春天的天气好，孩子你说呢？"老头子故意找话说。

"正是这么回事。"范·米克·康斯坦霞·库尔森小姐的回答有些含混，"威达普太太什么时候开始休假，爸爸？"

"我记得她说是从今天起休一星期。"库尔森先生答道。

范·米克·康斯坦霞小姐在窗口站了一会儿凝视着沐浴在下午温暖的阳光下的小公园。她是在

① adjoin /əˈdʒɔɪn/ v. 贴近，毗连

② venerable /ˈvenərəbl/ a. (因高龄、德行)令人肃然起敬的

③ lorgnette /lɔːˈnjet/ n. 带柄眼镜，带柄望远镜

④ obscurely /əbˈskjʊəlɪ/ ad. 晦涩地，费解地

potent weapons of **insidious**① May. With the cool pulses of a **virgin**② of Cologne she withstood the attack of the ethereal mildness. The arrows of the pleasant sunshine fell back, frostbitten, from the cold **panoply**③ of her unthrilled bosom. The odor of the flowers waked no soft sentiments in the unexplored recesses of her **dormant**④ heart. The chirp of the sparrows gave her a pain. She **mocked**⑤ at May.

But although Miss Coulson was proof against the season, she was keen enough to estimate its power. She knew that elderly men and thick-waisted women jumped as educated fleas in the ridiculous train of May, the merry mocker of the months. She had heard of foolish old gentlemen marrying their housekeepers before. What a **humiliating**⑥ thing, after all, was this feeling called love!

The next morning at 8 o'clock, when the iceman called, the cook told him that Miss Coulson wanted to see him in the basement.

"Well, ain't I the Olcott and Depew; not mentioning the first name at all? " said the iceman, admiringly, of himself.

As a concession he rolled his sleeves down, dropped his icehooks on a syringa and went back. When Miss Van Meeker Constantia Coulson addressed him he took off his hat.

"There is a rear entrance to this basement," said Miss Coulson, "which can be reached by driving into the vacant lot next door, where they are **excavating**⑦ for a building. I want you to bring in that way within two hours 1,000 pounds of ice. You may have to bring another man or two to help you. I will show you where I want it placed. I also want 1,000 pounds a day delivered the same way for the next four days. Your company may charge the ice on our regular bill. This is for your extra trouble."

① insidious /ɪnˈsɪdɪəs/ a. 暗中为害的

② virgin /ˈvɜːdʒɪn/ n. 处女

③ panoply /ˈpænəplɪ/ n. 全副盔甲

④ dormant /ˈdɔːmənt/ a. 睡眠状态的,静止的

⑤ mock /mɒk/ v. 嘲弄,嘲笑

⑥ humiliate /hjuːˈmɪlɪeɪt/ v. 羞辱

⑦ excavate /ˈekskəveɪt/ v. 挖掘,发掘

用植物学家的眼睛观察花，而花是狡猾的五月用以偷偷制服人的最厉害的武器。她的脉搏像科隆的处女一样波澜不惊，可见能抵挡和风的柔情。温暖的阳光的利箭射不进她冷冰冰的护胸甲胄，落到地上，也变凉了。她那颗沉睡的心还是个未知领域，花儿的芳香唤不起心中的温情。麻雀的叽喳叫只使她觉得难受。她冷对五月。

话说回来，尽管库尔森小姐叫五月奈何不得，她却能估量到五月的能耐。一年中的这个月最胡闹，坐上了五月的怪车，上了年纪的男人和粗腰身的女人会变成经过训练的跳蚤，叫蹦就蹦。她早听说过老糊涂娶女管家的事。把这种感情叫成爱情，多离奇！

第二天上午八点，卖冰的人来了。厨师对他说，库尔森小姐请他到地下室去一趟。

"哼，就不叫出名，谁还不知道我是奥尔科特—迪普公司？"卖冰人这样神气活现地炫耀着自己的身份。

然而他还是放下了袖子，把冰钩摆到注水器上，走了回来。范·米克·康斯坦霞·库尔森小姐对他说话时，他取下了帽子。

"这房子的地下室有个后门。"库尔森小姐说，"隔壁在挖地基建房子，你的车从那块空地上过就能走到后门。请你两小时内从后门送一千磅冰来。你还可以找一两个人帮忙。放冰的地点我会告诉你。明天也是一千磅，也从后门进，接连送四天。这些冰的钱照老办法付给你们公司。这点钱给你，就算有劳你了。"

Miss Coulson tendered a ten-dollar bill. The iceman bowed, and held his hat in his two hands behind him.

"Not if you'll excuse me, lady. It'll be a pleasure to fix things up for you any way you please."

Alas for May!

About noon Mr. Coulson knocked two glasses off his table, broke the spring of his bell and yelled for Higgins at the same time.

"Bring an axe," commanded Mr. Coulson, sardonically, "or send out for a quart of prussic acid, or have a policeman come in and shoot me. I'd rather that than be frozen to death."

"It does seem to be getting cool, Sir," said Higgins. "I hadn't noticed it before. I'll close the window, Sir."

"Do," said Mr. Coulson. "They call this spring, do they? If it keeps up long I'll go back to Palm Beach. House feels like a morgue."

Later Miss Coulson **dutifully**① came in to inquire how the gout was progressing.

"'Stantia," said the old man, "how is the weather outdoors?"

"Bright," answered Miss Coulson, "but chilly."

"Feels like the dead of winter to me," said Mr. Coulson.

"An instance," said Constantia, gazing **abstractedly** ② out the window, "of 'winter **lingering** ③ in the lap of spring,' though the **metaphor**④ is not in the most refined taste."

A little later she walked down by the side of the little park and on westward to Broadway to accomplish a little shopping.

A little later than that Mrs. Widdup entered the invalid's room.

"Did you ring, Sir?" she asked, **dimpling** ⑤ in many places. "I asked Higgins to go to the drug store, and I thought I heard your bell."

库尔森小姐拿出一张十美元钞票。卖冰人鞠了一躬，两手在身后抓着帽子。

"小姐，你这就用不着了。怎么办一切都听从小姐吩咐，我乐意效劳。"

五月真多怪事！

中午时分，库尔森先生把桌上的杯子掀下了两个，还按坏了铃的弹簧，一边扯开喉咙叫希金斯快来。

"快拿把斧头来，要不就叫人去买一夸脱氰酸，要不就喊警察把我毙啦！活活冻死还不如那样痛快。"库尔森先生下了莫名其妙的命令。

"老爷，天的确像在转冷。我刚才还没注意。我把窗关上吧。老爷。"希金斯说。

"快关！"库尔森先生说。"这种天还算得了春天吗？要这样冷下去，我回棕榈滩去。这屋子成太平间啦！"

库尔森小姐不愧为孝顺女儿，过一会儿进来了，问风湿痛有没有好些。

"斯坦霞，外面天气怎样？"老头问。

"大晴天，只是冷得很。"库尔森小姐答道。

"我看像是三九寒天。"库尔森先生说。

康斯坦霞茫然望着窗外，说："这就是有人说的'冬天赖在春天怀里'，但我看这样说算不得怎么高明。"

过了一会儿，她从小公园的侧面往西去百老汇，想买点东西。

她走后又过了一会儿，威达普太太来到风湿痛病人的房间。

"老爷，你按了铃，是吗？"她问，笑得满脸是酒窝，"我叫希金斯去药店买药了，好像听到

① dutifully /'dju:tɪfʊlɪ/ *ad.* 忠实地，尽职地

② abstractedly /æb'stræktɪdlɪ/ *ad.* 心不在焉地，走神地

③ linger /'lɪŋɡə/ *v.* 继续逗留，徘徊，流连

④ metaphor /'metəfə/ *n.* 隐喻

⑤ dimple /'dɪmpl/ *v.* 显现酒窝；起涟漪

"I did not," said Mr. Coulson.

"I'm afraid," said Mrs. Widdup, "I interrupted you sir, yesterday when you were about to say something."

"How comes it, Mrs. Widdup," said old man Coulson sternly, "that I find it so cold in this house?"

"Cold, Sir?" said the housekeeper, "why, now, since you speak of it it do seem cold in this room. But, outdoors it's as warm and fine as June, sir. And how this weather do seem to make one's heart jump out of one's shirt waist, sir. And the **ivy**① all leaved out on the side of the house, and the hand-organs playing, and the children dancing on the sidewalk — 'tis a great time for speaking out what's in the heart. You were saying yesterday, sir —"

"Woman!" roared Mr. Coulson; "you are a fool. I pay you to take care of this house. I am freezing to death in my own room, and you come in and **drivel**② to me about ivy and hand-organs. Get me an overcoat at once. See that all doors and windows are closed below. An old, fat, irresponsible, one-sided object like you **prating**③ about springtime and flowers in the middle of winter! When Higgins comes back, tell him to bring me a hot rum punch. And now get out!"

But who shall shame the bright face of May? Rogue though she be and disturber of sane men's peace, no wise virgins **cunning**④ nor cold storage shall make her bow her head in the bright **galaxy**⑤ of months.

Oh, yes, the story was not quite finished.

A night passed, and Higgins helped old man Coulson in the morning to his chair by the window. The cold of the room was gone. Heavenly odors and fragrant mildness entered.

In hurried Mrs. Widdup, and stood by his chair. Mr. Coulson

你按了铃。"

"我没按。"库尔森先生说。

威达普太太说："我怕昨天老爷像是要说什么话叫我岔开了。"

库尔森老头板着脸问："威达普太太，我觉得这屋子冷得厉害，这是怎么回事？"

"老爷觉得冷？"管家反问，"呀，真怪，老爷说这房子冷当真这房子就冷了。不过，外面有太阳，像六月天那么暖和，老爷。这天气真叫人心里有说不出的畅快。房子外边墙的藤长齐了叶子，有人拉起了手风琴，娃娃们在人行道上还跳舞呐。就这时候谈心里的事最合适。老爷，昨天你想说……"

"去你的！"库尔森先生吼了起来，"你这蠢货，我出钱是叫你把这屋子管好。坐在自己房子里我都快冻死了，你跑进来还只顾拉扯什么藤呀，手风琴呀。马上去给我把大衣拿来，把下面的门窗全部关上。大冷天的还唠叨什么春天，花，你这胖老婆子又不管用又糊涂！等希金斯回来叫他热点有酒的饮料来。你这就给我滚出去！"

然而，有谁能羞辱五月的笑脸呢？五月照旧诡计多端，惹得头脑清醒的人神魂颠倒。虽然多心计的姑娘狡诈，用了个冷窖从中作梗，五月并没有低下她的头，仍然胜过其他月份。

哦，对，故事还没有说完。

过了一夜，到第二天上午，希金斯把库尔森老头扶到窗边的椅上。房间里不冷了，人间天堂的各色气味与温馨的花香同时飘了进来。

突然威达普太太急急忙忙走进房站到他的椅

① ivy /'aɪvɪ/ *n.* 常春藤

② drivel /'drɪvl/ *v.* 说傻话，讲幼稚的无聊话

③ prate /preɪt/ *v.* 唠叨，胡扯

④ cunning /'kʌnɪŋ/ *a.* 狡猾的，奸诈的

⑤ galaxy /'gæləksɪ/ *n.* 银河；一群（出色的人或灿烂的事物）

reached his bony hand and grasped her plump one.

"Mrs. Widdup," he said, "this house would be no home without you. I have half a million dollars. If that and the true affection of a heart no longer in its youthful prime, but still not cold, could — "

"I found out what made it cold," said Mrs. Widdup, leanin' against his chair. "'Twas ice — tons of it — in the basement and in the furnace room, everywhere. I shut off the registers that it was coming through into your room, Mr. Coulson, poor soul! And now it's Maytime again."

"A true heart," went on old man Coulson, a little wanderingly, "that the springtime has brought to life again, and — but what will my daughter say, Mrs. Widdup? "

"Never fear, sir," said Mrs. Widdup, cheerfully. "Miss Coulson, she ran away with the iceman last night, sir! "

子边。库尔森先生伸出一只瘦骨嶙峋的手抓住她的圆滚滚的手说：

"威达普太太，这屋子没有了你就不会成为一家人家。我有五十万块钱。要是这笔钱还顶用，要是一颗真有感情的心尽管不像当年，可是还没有冷，还能……"

"我知道了为什么昨天冷得厉害，"威达普太太靠在他椅上，"是冰在作怪，有好几吨，地下室里摆着，客厅里摆着，没哪儿没摆着。我把往你房间里灌冷气的进口全关死啦！库尔森先生，真作践人啦！现在好了，又是五月天。"

库尔森老头只顾说自己的："心里的真情是春天唤醒的——不过，威达普太太，我女儿会怎么说呢？"

"老爷别担心，库尔森小姐昨天晚上跟着卖冰的人跑啦！"威达普太太喜形于色地说。

这是一个关于幻想的故事。

　　沉湎在爱情幻想中的人儿，会突然注意起自己的穿着，为一点小事耳热心跳，为一个小把戏得逞而窃喜，为一个小期待落空而失落……

　　然而不少时候，美好的幻想会在现实中碰壁，甚至碰得鼻青脸肿。也许你会懊恼不已，痛骂自己的愚蠢。不过没用的，只要你还有憧憬，还有期待，那么幻想就不会停止。

Witches' Loaves

Miss Martha Meacham kept the little bakery on the corner (the one where you go up three steps, and the bell **tinkles**① when you open the door).

Miss Martha was forty, her **bank-book**② showed a **credit**③ of two thousand dollars, and she possessed two false teeth and a sympathetic heart. Many people have married whose chances to do so were much **inferior**④ to Miss Martha's.

Two or three times a week a customer came in in whom she began to take an interest. He was a middle-aged man, wearing spectacles and a brown beard trimmed to a careful point.

He spoke English with a strong German accent. His clothes were worn and **darned**⑤ in places, and **wrinkled**⑥ and baggy in others. But he looked neat, and had very good manners.

He always bought two loaves of stale bread. Fresh bread was five cents a loaf. Stale ones were two for five. Never did he call for anything but stale bread.

Once Miss Martha saw a red and brown stain on his fingers. She was sure then that he was an artist and very poor. No doubt he lived in a

多情女的面包

① tinkle /'tɪŋkl/ *v.* 发叮当
声,发丁零声

② bank-book /'bæŋkbʊk/ *n.*
银行存折

③ credit /'kredɪt/ *n.* 存款

④ inferior /ɪn'fɪərɪə（r）/ *a.*
低于……的

⑤ darn /daːn/ *v.* 织补

⑥ wrinkled /'rɪŋkld/ *a.* 有褶
皱的

马萨·米查姆小姐的小面包店开在路口,就是
你得上三级台阶,打开门后铃会响的那一家。

马萨小姐四十岁,有两千美元存款,镶着两
颗假牙,生来一副好心肠。偏偏有许多条件大不
如马萨小姐的人倒先结了婚。

有位顾客一星期来两三次,马萨小姐对这人
产生了兴趣。这人是中年人,戴副眼睛,下巴上
棕色的长胡须修得溜尖。

这人说话带浓重的德国口音,衣服好几处穿
破了,打了补丁,没破的地方不是皱就是鼓,但
一身收拾得倒干净,而且彬彬有礼。

他每次只买两块陈面包,新鲜的要五分钱一
块,而陈面包五美分可以买两块。除了陈面包,
别的东西他从不问津。

有一次,马萨小姐发现他手指上沾了一点棕
红色颜料,便断定他是位画家,而且穷得很。不
用说,他住的是小阁楼,在阁楼里作画,啃陈面
包,马萨小姐店里好吃的东西只能空想想。

garret, where he painted pictures and ate stale bread and thought of the good things to eat in Miss Martha's bakery.

Often when Miss Martha sat down to her chops and light rolls and jam and tea she would sigh, and wish that the gentle-mannered artist might share her tasty meal instead of eating his dry crust in that draughty attic. Miss Martha's heart, as you have been told, was a sympathetic one.

In order to test her theory as to his occupation, she brought from her room one day a painting that she had bought at a sale, and set it against the shelves behind the bread counter.

It was a Venetian scene. A splendid marble palazzio (so it said on the picture) stood in the foreground — or rather forewater. For the rest there were gondolas (with the lady trailing her hand in the water), clouds, sky, and chiaro-oscuro in plenty. No artist could fail to notice it.

Two days afterward the customer came in.

"Two loafs of stale bread, if you blease.

"You haf here a fine bicture, madame," he said while she was wrapping up the bread.

"Yes? " says Miss Martha, **reveling**[①] in her own cunning. "I do so admire art and" (no, it would not do to say "artists" thus early) "and paintings," she **substituted**[②]. "You think it is a good picture? "

"Der balance," said the customer, "is not in good drawing. Der bairspective of it is not true. Goot morning, madame."

He took his bread, bowed, and hurried out.

Yes, he must be an artist. Miss Martha took the picture back to her room.

How gentle and kindly his eyes shone behind his spectacles! What

　　马萨小姐在吃排骨、面包卷、果酱和喝茶时，常唉声叹气，惦念着那位在小阁楼里啃硬面包的文质彬彬的画家，就可惜他不能来分享她的佳肴。前面已经说过，马萨小姐生来一副好心肠。

　　为了证实自己对他的身份猜得是否正确，马萨小姐把她在一次拍卖时买来的一幅画从房里取了出来，挂到柜台后的架子上。

　　这是一幅威尼斯风景画，画了座富丽堂皇的大理石宫殿（画上是这样标明的），建在水边。水上荡着几叶轻舟，一位女郎用手轻轻拨着水。另外还画了云、天空，大量使用了明暗对比法。如果是画家，绝不会注意不到。

　　两天后这位顾客又来了。

　　"请拿两块陈面包。"

　　马萨小姐包面包时，他又说话了。"小姐，你借（这）画很裱（漂）亮嘛！"

　　"当真？"马萨小姐说，暗自得意巧计成功，"我喜欢美术，喜欢画。"（现在说"喜欢画家"为时过早。）接着她换了话题问："你觉得这画画得好吗？"

　　"不够协调。透戏（视）法运用得不合戏（适）。介（再）见，小姐！"顾客道。

　　他拿起面包，一鞠躬，匆匆走了。

　　没错，他准是画家。马萨小姐把画又拿回她房里。

　　他眼镜后的两只眼多温和、善良呵！前额长得真宽！一眼能看出透视法运用不当，却只能啃陈面包过日子！然而，往往天才在得到承认之前

① revel /'revəl/ v. 陶醉，着迷

② substitute /'sʌbstɪtjuːt/ v. 用……代替，代以

a broad brow he had! To be able to judge perspective at a glance —
and to live on stale bread! But genius often has to struggle before it is
recognized.

What a thing it would be for art and perspective if genius were
backed by two thousand dollars in bank, a bakery, and a sympathetic
heart to — But these were day-dreams, Miss Martha.

Often now when he came he would chat for a while across the
showcase①. He seemed to **crave**② Miss Martha's cheerful words.

He kept on buying stale bread. Never a cake, never a pie, never
one of her delicious Sally Lunns.

She thought he began to look thinner and discouraged. Her heart
ached to add something good to eat to his **meagre**③ purchase, but her
courage failed at the act. She did not dare **affront**④ him. She knew the
pride of artists.

Miss Martha took to wearing her blue-dotted silk waist behind the
counter. In the back room she cooked a mysterious compound of quince
seeds and borax. Ever so many people use it for the complexion.

One day the customer came in as usual, laid his nickel on the
showcase, and called for his stale loaves. While Miss Martha was
reaching for them there was a great **tooting**⑤ and **clanging**⑥, and a fire-
engine came **lumbering**⑦ past.

The customer hurried to the door to look, as any one will. Suddenly
inspired, Miss Martha seized the opportunity.

On the bottom shelf behind the counter was a pound of fresh butter
that the dairyman had left ten minutes before. With a bread knife Miss
Martha made a deep slash in each of the stale loaves, inserted a
generous quantity of butter, and pressed the loaves tight again.

When the customer turned once more she was tying the paper

不得不艰苦奋斗。

如果天才有两千美元银行存款，一个面包店，一个满心同情他的人来……那么艺术与透视法将会有多辉煌的成就！然而，马萨小姐，别想入非非了。

自那次以后，他常会隔着货柜跟她闲聊几句。他似乎爱听马萨小姐的热心话。

① showcase /ˈʃəʊkeɪs/ n. （商店的）货柜
② crave /kreɪv/ v. 渴望得到，迫切需要

他只要陈面包，从没买过一块蛋糕，一块肉馅饼，一块可口的莎伦饼。

她觉得他越来越瘦、越来越没精神了。马萨小姐过意不去，想在他买的便宜货里加点好吃的，却又鼓不起勇气动手。她不敢贸然。她理解艺术家的自尊。

③ meagre /ˈmiːgə/ a. （尤指食物）质量差的，粗劣的
④ affront /əˈfrʌnt/ v. 勇敢地面对

马萨小姐换了件有蓝圆点的丝绸衣服站柜台。她还在后房里将榅桲子和硼砂放在一起熬，其汁有神奇效用，现在仍有许多人用此来美容。

有一天，那位顾客又来了，把一个五美分的镍币往柜台上一放，照旧买陈面包。就在马萨小姐伸手拿面包时，街上响起了哨声和叮叮当当的铃声，一辆消防车轰鸣而过。

⑤ tooting /ˈtuːtɪŋ/ n. 汽笛声
⑥ clanging /ˈklæŋɪŋ/ n. （金属相击的）铿锵声，当当声
⑦ lumber /ˈlʌmbə/ v. 笨拙地（费力）行进

遇到这种事谁都会站到门口看看，那位顾客也不例外。马萨小姐灵机一动，抓住良机。

柜台后的底层货架上放着一磅新鲜奶油，刚送来十分钟。马萨小姐拿起面包刀把两块陈面包都深深划了一刀，塞进好些奶油后紧紧捏拢。

等那位顾客再走回柜台时，她已经在包面包了。

around them.

When he had gone, after an unusually pleasant little chat, Miss Martha smiled to herself, but not without a slight fluttering of the heart.

Had she been too bold? Would he **take offense**①? But surely not. There was no language of **edibles** ②. Butter was no emblem of **unmaidenly**③ forwardness.

For a long time that day her mind dwelt on the subject. She imagined the scene when he should discover her little deception.

He would lay down his brushes and palette. There would stand his easel with the picture he was painting in which the perspective was beyond criticism.

He would prepare for his luncheon of dry bread and water. He would **slice**④ into a loaf — ah!

Miss Martha blushed. Would he think of the hand that placed it there as he ate? Would he —

The front door bell **jangled**⑤ viciously. Somebody was coming in, making a great deal of noise.

Miss Martha hurried to the front. Two men were there. One was a young man smoking a pipe — a man she had never seen before. The other was her artist.

His face was very red, his hat was on the back of his head, his hair was wildly **rumpled** ⑥. He clinched his two fists and shook them **ferociously**⑦ at Miss Martha. At Miss Martha.

"Dummkopf! " he shouted with extreme loudness; and then "Tausendonfer! " or something like it in German.

The young man tried to draw him away.

"I vill not go," he said angrily, "else I shall told her."

He made a **bass drum**⑧ of Miss Martha's counter.

他闲谈了几句，话显得格外动听，然后走了。马萨小姐心中暗笑，但也不是没有一点忐忑不安。

她是不是太胆大妄为？他会生气吗？当然不会。吃的东西什么也说明不了，况且送一点奶油也不算姑娘家有失体统的事。

这天她心上老牵挂着这件事。她想象着他发现上了个小小的当后的情形。

他会放下笔和调色板。画架上搁着他在画的一张画，当然透视法用得是无可挑剔。

他打算吃午饭了，还是干面包和开水。等他切开面包——哟！

马萨小姐脸红了。吃面包时他会惦念起在面包里打了埋伏的人吗？他会……

前门的铃乱响起来，有人进来了，哇哇乱叫着。

马萨小姐连忙赶到店堂里。进来了两个人。一个是年轻人，叼着根烟斗，她以前从没见过。另一个是她关心的画家。

他的脸涨得通红，帽子罩在后脑勺上，头发像一堆乱草。他攥紧两只拳头，向着马萨小姐恶狠狠挥。竟然向马萨小姐挥！

"Dummkopf!"他的叫声震得人耳发麻，然后又是，"Tausendonfer!"之类的话，像是德语。

年轻人使劲拽住他。

"我不走，"他气冲冲说，"要找她算将（账）！"

他把马萨小姐的柜台当大鼓敲。

① take offense 生气,见怪
② edible /'edɪbl/ n. 食物
③ unmaidenly /ʌn'meɪdənlɪ/ a. 不适合少女身份的
④ slice /slaɪs/ v. 把……切成片
⑤ jangle /'dʒæŋgl/ v. 发出丁零当啷声
⑥ rumple /rʌmpl/ v. 弄乱
⑦ ferociously /fə'rəʊʃəslɪ/ ad. 狂暴地
⑧ bass drum 大鼓

"You haf shpoilt me," he cried, his blue eyes **blazing**[①] behind his spectacles. "I vill tell you. You vas von meddingsome old cat! "

Miss Martha leaned weakly against the shelves and laid one hand on her blue-dotted silk waist. The young man took the other by the collar.

"Come on," he said, "you've said enough." He dragged the angry one out at the door to the sidewalk, and then came back.

"Guess you ought to be told, ma'am," he said, "what the **row**[②] is about. That's Blumberger. He's an architectural draftsman. I work in the same office with him.

"He's been working hard for three months drawing a plan for a new city hall. It was a prize competition. He finished inking the lines yesterday. You know, a draftsman always makes his drawing in pencil first. When it's done he rubs out the pencil lines with handfuls of stale bread crumbs. That's better than India rubber.

"Blumberger's been buying the bread here. Well, to-day — well, you know, ma'am, that butter isn't — well, Blumberger's plan isn't good for anything now except to cut up into railroad sandwiches."

Miss Martha went into the back room. She took off the blue-dotted silk waist and put on the old brown serge she used to wear. Then she poured the quince seed and borax mixture out of the window into the ash can.

① blaze /bleɪz/ v. 熊熊燃烧

"你把我委（毁）啦！"他大叫着，眼镜后的两只蓝眼睛直冒火，"你定脚（听着），谁叫你多官（管）闲戏（事）来脚（着）！"

马萨小姐有气无力地斜靠在货架上，一只手按在蓝圆点丝绸衣上。年轻人拽着另一个人的衣领。

"得了吧，你也说够了。"他说，把大发雷霆的人拖到门外，然后自己又走回来。

"小姐，我想还是应该告诉你为什么他大吵大闹。"他说，"这人姓布卢姆伯格，是建筑设计师。我与他在同一个办公室。"

② row /raʊ/ n. 吵嚷，吵闹

"他辛辛苦苦干了三个月，为新市政大楼画图纸，是要参加比赛夺奖的，用墨水描线条昨天才描完。你不知道，设计师画图总是先用铅笔打草稿，定稿以后用陈面包屑擦去铅笔印，比用橡皮擦的效果好。

"布卢姆伯格老来这儿买面包。嗯——今天，嗯，今天，你知道，小姐，那奶油不——嗯，布卢姆伯格的图纸完全成了废纸。"

马萨小姐回到后房，脱下有蓝圆点的丝绸衣，换上那件以前常穿的棕色旧哔叽衫，把榅桲子和硼砂熬的汁倒进了窗外的垃圾箱里。

这是一个关于人生际遇的故事。

对于某些人来说，时光和境遇并不那么仁慈，坎坷的命运总在考验他们的耐心，相比奋斗，毕竟堕落来得更容易些。

索彼就是这样一个倒霉蛋。他曾享受过温暖、甜蜜，有过朋友，产生过抱负，却偶然跌入堕落的深坑，等他想回头时，命运却与他开起了玩笑。

这，就是人生的无奈吧。

The Cop and the Anthem

On his bench in **Madison Square**[1] Soapy moved uneasily. When wild geese **honk**[2] high of nights, and when women without sealskin coats grow kind to their husbands, and when Soapy moves uneasily on his bench in the park, you may know that winter is near **at hand**[3].

A dead leaf fell in Soapy's lap. That was Jack Frost's card. Jack is kind to the regular denizens of Madison Square, and gives fair warning of his annual call. At the corners of four streets he hands his pasteboard to the North Wind, footman of the mansion of All Outdoors, so that the inhabitants thereof may make ready.

Soapy's mind became **cognizant**[4] of the fact that the time had come for him to resolve himself into a singular Committee of Ways and Means to provide against the coming rigor. And therefore he moved uneasily on his bench.

The **hibernatorial**[5] ambitions of Soapy were not of the highest. In them there were no considerations of Mediterranean cruises, of **soporific**[6] Southern skies drifting in the Vesuvian Bay. Three months on the Island was what his soul craved. Three months of assured board and bed and **congenial**[7] company, safe from **Boreas**[8] and bluecoats, seemed to Soapy

警察与圣歌

① Madison Square 麦迪逊广场

② honk /hɔŋk/ v. (雁)叫

③ at hand 在手边

④ cognizant /'kɒɡnɪzənt/ a. 知道的,认识的
⑤ hibernatorial /'haɪbəneɪ'tɔrɪəl/ a. 过冬的
⑥ soporific /ˌsəʊpə'rɪfɪk/ a. 睡眠的,催眠的
⑦ congenial /kən'dʒiːnɪəl/ a. 意气相投的,情投意合的
⑧ Boreas /'bɔrɪæs/ n. [希神] 北风神

索彼在麦迪逊广场的长凳上总不得安稳。等到夜晚听到雁群拉大嗓门叫唤时,等到那些没有海豹皮大衣的女人对丈夫殷勤起来时,也等到索彼在公园的凳子上总不得安稳时,你就知道,冬天已指日可待。

一片落叶飘到索彼的膝上。这是冬先生送的名片。冬先生对麦迪逊广场的常客素来体贴,每年来前总要彬彬有礼地打个招呼。交叉路口处他的片子是叫北风送的,因为风是露天大厦的看门人,这一来睡街头的人就会有所准备。

索彼的心里已经有数,知道严冬逼近,他得单枪匹马想办法对付。所以他在凳上不得安稳了。

索彼过冬的打算并非什么宏图大略,他既没想去地中海游弋,也没想到南国休眠,在维苏威湾泛舟。他只巴望能到岛上待三个月。三个月里不愁吃住,有合得来的伙伴,北风吹不着,警察不找麻烦,他就谢天谢地,心满意足。

· 105 ·

the essence of things desirable.

For years the hospitable Blackwell's had been his winter quarters. Just as his more fortunate fellow New Yorkers had bought their tickets to Palm Beach and the Riviera each winter, so Soapy had made his humble arrangements for his annual **hegira**① to the Island. And now the time was come. On the previous night three Sabbath newspapers, distributed beneath his coat, about his ankles and over his lap, had failed to repulse the cold as he slept on his bench near the spurting fountain in the ancient square. So the Island **loomed**② big and timely in Soapy's mind. He scorned the provisions made in the name of charity for the city's dependents. In Soapy's opinion the Law was more benign than **Philanthropy**③. There was an endless round of institutions, municipal and eleemosynary, on which he might set out and receive **lodging**④ and food **accordant**⑤ with the simple life. But to one of Soapy's proud spirit the gifts of charity are **encumbered**⑥. If not in coin you must pay in **humiliation**⑦ of spirit for every benefit received at the hands of philanthropy. As Caesar had his Brutus, every bed of charity must have its toll of a bath, every loaf of bread its **compensation**⑧ of a private and personal **inquisition**⑨. Wherefore it is better to be a guest of the law, which though conducted by rules, does not meddle unduly with a gentleman's private affairs.

Soapy, having decided to go to the Island, at once set about accomplishing his desire. There were many easy ways of doing this. The pleasantest was to dine **luxuriously**⑩ at some expensive restaurant; and then, after declaring insolvency, be handed over quietly and without uproar to a policeman. An accommodating magistrate would do the rest.

Soapy left his bench and **strolled**⑪ out of the square and across the

好些年冬天他待在大方好客的布莱克韦尔监狱。比他命好的纽约人每年冬天买票去棕榈滩和里维埃拉，而索彼可怜巴巴，年年只能当穆罕默德，逃亡岛上。现在又到这种时候了。昨天夜里，他睡在这个老广场靠喷泉的长凳上，用三份星期天的报纸垫在大衣里，盖住腿、脚，还是挡不住寒气。所以那个避难岛又浮现到索彼的脑海里。市里对无家可归的人本有一些救济，即所谓"施舍"，可他瞧不上眼。在索彼看来，"博爱"的慈悲之心还比不过法律。市里办的和慈善团体办的机构比比皆是，只要他肯进，有吃有住，能过规范的简朴生活。但索彼性傲，不肯要别人发善心相助。出自慈善家之手的馈赠，虽说你不破钞即可得，但要以心灵受屈辱为代价，件件如此。恺撒尚且没逃过布鲁特斯之手；哪个要住慈善机构的床，非得先把一身洗干净不可；哪个要吃块面包，就得让人盘问自己的隐秘。因此还不如做一趟牢中客，固然监狱中规矩严格，但毕竟不会瞎干预君子的私事。

索彼一旦决定了去那岛上，便着手实现他的打算。要办到办法又多又容易。最惬意的是到哪家高档餐馆美餐一顿，吃完直截了当说钱已用得精光，让人往警察局一送，干干脆脆，没声没响。往下的事自有好说话的法官料理。

索彼从凳上起身，走出广场，穿过百老汇与第五大道相交处老大一块平坦的柏油路口。他转进百老汇，在一家漂亮的咖啡馆前停了下来，这

---

① hegira /ˈhedʒɪrə/ n. 希吉拉（公元622年穆罕默德从麦加到麦地那的逃亡），逃亡

② loom /luːm/ v. 隐约地出现，阴森地逼近

③ philanthropy /fɪˈlænθrəpɪ/ n. 博爱，慈善

④ lodging /ˈlɒdʒɪŋ/ n. 寄宿，借宿

⑤ accordant /əˈkɔːdənt/ a. 一致的，和谐的

⑥ encumber /ɪnˈkʌmbə/ v. 妨碍，拖累

⑦ humiliation /hjuːˌmɪlɪˈeɪʃən/ n. 丢脸，羞辱，蒙羞

⑧ compensation /ˌkɒmpenˈseɪʃən/ n. 补偿，弥补，赔偿

⑨ inquisition /ˌɪnkwɪˈzɪʃən/ n. 调查，查究

⑩ luxuriously /lʌgˈʒʊərɪəslɪ/ ad. 奢侈地，豪华地

⑪ stroll /strəʊl/ v. 散步，溜达，缓步走

level sea of asphalt, where Broadway and Fifth Avenue flow together. Up Broadway he turned, and halted at a **glittering**① cafe, where are gathered together nightly the choicest products of the grape, the silkworm and the protoplasm.

Soapy had confidence in himself from the lowest button of his vest upward. He was shaven, and his coat was decent and his neat black, ready-tied four-in-hand had been presented to him by a lady **missionary**② on Thanksgiving Day. If he could reach a table in the restaurant unsuspected success would be his. The portion of him that would show above the table would raise no doubt in the waiter's mind. A roasted **mallard**③ duck, thought Soapy, would be about the thing — with a bottle of Chablis, and then Camembert, a demi-tasse and a cigar. One dollar for the cigar would be enough. The total would not be so high as to call forth any supreme **manifestation**④ of revenge from the cafe management; and yet the meat would leave him filled and happy for the journey to his winter **refuge**⑤.

But as Soapy set foot inside the restaurant door the head waiter's eye fell upon his frayed trousers and decadent shoes. Strong and ready hands turned him about and conveyed him in silence and haste to the sidewalk and averted the ignoble fate of the **menaced**⑥ mallard.

Soapy turned off Broadway. It seemed that his route to the coveted island was not to be an **epicurean**⑦ one. Some other way of entering limbo must be thought of.

At a corner of Sixth Avenue electric lights and cunningly displayed wares behind plate-glass made a shop window **conspicuous**⑧. Soapy took a cobblestone and dashed it through the glass. People came running around the corner, a policeman in the lead. Soapy stood still, with his hands in his pockets, and smiled at the sight of brass buttons.

儿夜夜摆着最上等的美酒佳肴，坐着衣冠华丽的宾客和社会中坚人物。

从背心最下一颗纽扣往上看，索彼觉得自己的仪表准没问题。脸刮得干干净净，上衣总算体面，还打了一根干净的黑色活结领带，那是感恩节一位女传教士送的。如果他没引起人怀疑，能走到这家店的一张桌子边，那就稳操胜券了。露出桌子的上半身叫服务员看不出破绽。索彼想，要只烤野鸭差不多，外带一瓶法国白葡萄酒和法国名干酪，一杯黑咖啡，一根雪茄。一美元一根的雪茄足够了。几件东西加起来钱不会太多，太多了店老板会狠狠教训他一顿的。吃完了喝完了他也就饱了，高高兴兴地上路，去他过冬的避难所。

没承想索彼一踏进店门，领班服务员一眼就瞧见了他那已经磨破的裤子和不成体统的鞋子。他被一双又有力又利落的手扳转身，没声没响推出来，那只野鸭也就逃脱了遭暗算的厄运。

索彼没再走百老汇路，觉得美餐一顿白食不是个办法，到岛上去此路不通，进那个既非天堂又非地狱的地方得另想办法。

走到第六大道的一个路口，只见一家商店的玻璃橱窗电灯通亮，商品琳琅满目。索彼捡起块铺路石把玻璃砸碎了。行人从两边涌过来；跑在前头的正是个警察。索彼站着没动，双手插在衣袋里，望着那衣上有铜纽扣的人直笑。

① glittering /'glɪtərɪŋ/ a. 闪闪发光的,闪烁的

② missionary /'mɪʃənərɪ/ n. 传教士

③ mallard /'mæləd/ a. 绿头鸭

④ manifestation /ˌmænɪfes'teɪʃən/ n. 显示,表明

⑤ refuge /'refjuːdʒ/ n. 躲避,庇护

⑥ menace /'menɪs/ v. 威胁,恐吓;危及

⑦ epicurean /ˌepɪkjʊ'riːən/ a. 好美食的,爱奢侈享受的

⑧ conspicuous /kən'spɪkjʊəs/ a. 明显的,显著的

"Where's the man that done that? " inquired the officer excitedly.

"Don't you figure out that I might have had something to do with it? " said Soapy, not without **sarcasm**①, but friendly, as one greets good fortune.

The policeman's mind refused to accept Soapy even as a clue. Men who smash windows do not remain to **parley**② with the law's **minions**③. They **take to their heels**④. The policeman saw a man half way down the block running to catch a car. With drawn club he joined in the pursuit. Soapy, with **disgust**⑤ in his heart, **loafed**⑥ along, twice unsuccessful.

On the opposite side of the street was a restaurant of no great pretensions. It catered to large appetites and modest purses. Its **crockery**⑦ and atmosphere were thick; its soup and napery thin. Into this place Soapy took his accusive shoes and telltale trousers without challenge. At a table he sat and consumed beefsteak, **flapjacks**⑧, doughnuts and pie. And then to the waiter he betrayed the fact that the minutest coin and himself were strangers.

"Now, get busy and call a cop," said Soapy. "And don't keep a gentleman waiting."

"No cop for youse," said the waiter, with a voice like butter cakes and an eye like the cherry in a Manhattan cocktail. "Hey, Con! "

Neatly upon his left ear on the **callous**⑨ pavement two waiters pitched Soapy. He arose, joint by joint, as a carpenter's rule opens, and beat the dust from his clothes. Arrest seemed but a rosy dream. The Island seemed very far away. A policeman who stood before a drug store two doors away laughed and walked down the street.

Five blocks Soapy travelled before his courage permitted him to woo capture again. This time the opportunity presented what he fatuously termed to himself a "cinch." A young woman of a modest and pleasing

"干这事的家伙跑到哪儿去了?"警察气喘吁吁地问。

"难道你就不怀疑我?"索彼反问,声气里听得出带点儿挖苦,然而笑容可掬,像是在迎候好运道。

警察根本没怀疑上索彼。谁砸了橱窗都不会站着等警察抓,会拔腿就跑的。警察发现半条马路开外,有人跑着赶一辆车,便拿着警棍追。索彼虽满心瞧不起他,但还是走了,第二次也没达到目的。

马路对过有家餐馆不太气派,是为那些食量大而钱包小的人开的,餐具厚重,空气污浊,汤稀稀拉拉,餐巾布薄薄一层。索彼进这种地方穿着不像样的鞋和露出穷酸相的裤子是没人阻拦的。他坐到一张桌边,享用了牛排、烙饼、油煎卷还有馅饼。吃完他对服务员道出了实情:他身无分文。

索彼说:"你去叫警察吧,别让你大爷久等。"

"用不着叫警察,"服务员说,声气柔和,眼里的火星却直往外冒,"来呀,康!"

两名服务员抓着索彼一推,他的左耳首先着地,哐当摔倒在硬邦邦的人行道上。他一节一节弯动着关节站起来,像是个木匠一段一段地打开曲尺,然后拍干净身上的灰土。想叫警察抓起来似乎也是做美梦,到避难岛看来还路漫漫。站在相隔两家的药店门外的一名警察打了两声哈哈,巡马路去了。

索彼走过五个路口才算恢复勇气,又追求起警察来。这一次他异想天开,以为有十拿九稳的

① sarcasm /'sɑːkæzəm/ n. 讽刺,挖苦,嘲笑

② parley /'pɑːlɪ/ v. 会谈,谈判

③ minion /'mɪnjən/ n. 宠儿,宠仆,奴才

④ take to one's heels 逃走

⑤ disgust /dɪs'ɡʌst/ n. 作呕;厌恶

⑥ loaf /ləʊf/ v. 游荡,闲逛

⑦ crockery /'krɒkərɪ/ n. 陶器,瓦器

⑧ flapjack /'flæpdʒæk/ n. 烙饼

⑨ callous /'kæləs/ a. 冷酷无情的

guise was standing before a show window gazing with sprightly interest at its display of shaving mugs and **inkstands**①, and two yards from the window a large policeman of severe **demeanor**② leaned against a water plug.

It was Soapy's design to assume the role of the **despicable**③ and execrated "masher." The refined and elegant appearance of his victim and the **contiguity**④ of the **conscientious**⑤ cop encouraged him to believe that he would soon feel the pleasant official clutch upon his arm that would insure his winter quarters on the right little, tight little isle.

Soapy straightened the lady missionary's readymade tie, dragged his shrinking cuffs into the open, set his hat at a killing cant and **sidled**⑥ toward the young woman. He made eyes at her, was taken with sudden coughs and "hems," smiled, **smirked**⑦ and went **brazenly**⑧ through the **impudent**⑨ and **contemptible**⑩ **litany**⑪ of the "masher." With half an eye Soapy saw that the policeman was watching him fixedly. The young woman moved away a few steps, and again bestowed her absorbed attention upon the shaving mugs. Soapy followed, boldly stepping to her side, raised his hat and said:

"Ah there, Bedelia! Don't you want to come and play in my yard?"

The policeman was still looking. The persecuted young woman had but to **beckon**⑫ a finger and Soapy would be practically en route for his **insular**⑬ haven. Already he imagined he could feel the cozy warmth of the station-house. The young woman faced him and, stretching out a hand, caught Soapy's coat sleeve.

"Sure, Mike," she said joyfully, "if you'll blow me to a pail of suds. I'd have spoke to you sooner, but the cop was watching."

With the young woman playing the clinging ivy to his oak, Soapy walked past the policeman overcome with gloom. He seemed doomed to

① inkstand /'ɪŋkstænd/ n. 墨
水瓶架
② demeanor /dɪ'miːnə/ n 行
为,风度

③ despicable /'despɪkəbl/
a. 可鄙的,卑劣的
④ contiguity /ˌkɒntɪ'gjuːɪtɪ/
n. 临近;接触
⑤ conscientious
/ˌkɒnʃɪ'enʃəs/ a. 凭良心
的,认真的

⑥ sidle /'saɪdl/ v. 侧身而行
⑦ smirk /'smɜːk/ v. 傻笑,假
笑
⑧ brazenly /breɪzənlɪ/ ad. 脸
皮厚地,无耻地
⑨ impudent /'ɪmpjʊdənt/ a.
厚颜无耻的,放肆的
⑩ contemptible
/kən'temptəbl/ a. 可鄙
的,不屑一顾的
⑪ litany /lɪtənɪ/ n. 枯燥冗长
的陈述

⑫ beckon /'bekən/ v. 向……
示意,召唤
⑬ insular /'ɪnsjʊlə/ a. 海岛
的,狭隘的

机会。一家商店的橱窗前站着位模样端庄可爱的年轻女郎,在津津有味地看里面摆的刮脸杯和墨水瓶架。离橱窗两码处站着位威严的大个子警察,背靠在消防龙头上。

索彼的方案是扮演一次惹人嫌遭人骂的"骚公鸡"。他瞄准的人儿文雅高贵,近在咫尺的警察忠于职守,使他信心十足,肯定会让警察扭住胳膊。这正是他求之不得的,只要一扭他过冬就不用愁,可以上那个小岛,那个不缺吃穿的安乐岛。

索彼把他那女教士送的领带结整平,缩进去了的衣袖扯出来,帽子歪戴得不像话,轻手轻脚朝那姑娘走。他又是向她飞媚眼,又是无缘无故地咳嗽,又是清嗓门,一下子微笑,一下子又傻笑,骚公鸡那套可鄙可恶的伎俩,他厚起脸皮要了个够。索彼斜眼一瞧,果见警察在盯着他看。女郎挪开几步,又聚精会神看着刮脸杯。索彼跟了过去,竟然挨到了她身边,掀了掀帽子,说:

"是你呀,贝德丽娅。到我家玩玩,行吗?"

警察还在看着。被纠缠的姑娘只要弯一弯小指头,索彼就可以住到他岛上的避难所了。他想得真美,仿佛警察局的舒舒服服的暖气都能感觉到了。姑娘转过脸来,伸出一只手,抓着索彼的衣袖。

"那当然,迈克。不过,你得请我喝杯啤酒。"她喜气洋洋说,"我本早想对你说话,就怪警察在死盯着。"

索彼大失所望,被那年轻女郎挽着从警察身

liberty.

At the next corner he shook off his companion and ran. He halted in the district where by night are found the lightest streets, hearts, vows and librettos. Women in furs and men in greatcoats moved gaily in the wintry air. A sudden fear seized Soapy that some dreadful **enchantment**① had rendered him immune to arrest. The thought brought a little of panic upon it, and when he came upon another policeman lounging grandly in front of a transplendent theatre he caught at the immediate straw of disorderly conduct.

On the sidewalk Soapy began to yell drunken **gibberish**② at the top of his harsh voice. He danced, howled, raved and otherwise disturbed the welkin.

The policeman **twirled**③ his club, turned his back to Soapy and remarked to a citizen.

"'Tis one of them Yale lads celebratin' the goose egg they give to the Hartford College. Noisy; but no harm. We've instructions to lave them be."

Disconsolate, Soapy ceased his unavailing racket. Would never a policeman lay hands on him? In his fancy the Island seemed an **unattainable**④ Arcadia. He buttoned his thin coat against the chilling wind.

In a cigar store he saw a well-dressed man lighting a cigar at a swinging light. His silk umbrella he had set by the door on entering. Soapy stepped inside, secured the umbrella and sauntered off with it slowly. The man at the cigar light followed hastily.

"My umbrella," he said, sternly.

"Oh, is it? " sneered Soapy, adding insult to **petit**⑤ **larceny**⑥. "Well, why don't you call a policeman? I took it. Your umbrella!

边走过，就像树上缠了根常春藤。监狱似乎与他无缘。

拐了一个弯后他甩开那女的撒腿就跑，直跑到一个街上灯光最亮的地段。入夜以后，上这里的人有来找称心事儿的，有来赌咒发誓的，有来看歌剧的。穿长大衣和裘皮衣的男男女女不怕冬天的寒气，来来去去走得欢快。突然，索彼担心起来，怕自己中了什么邪，就不能让警察抓去。他想着想着有点胆寒，但就在这时又遇上了一名警察。那人在家剧院前站着，挺精神。使他立即捞到了根救命稻草，想起有"扰乱治安行为"这一条。

索彼扯开粗嗓门，在人行道上醉汉般乱叫起来。他跳着，喊着，胡说八道着，无所不为，搅得连天公也不安宁。

警察甩着警棍，背转身干脆不瞧索彼，还对一个人说：

"那是耶鲁大学的学生，庆祝他们赛球给了哈德福学院一个大鸭蛋。就叫唤叫唤，没事。上头有交代，别理他们。"

索彼泄了气，徒劳无益的事只好作罢。难道不会有警察来逮他吗？他认为那个岛有些可望而不可即。风刮得冷飕飕，他把薄薄的上衣的纽扣扣上了。

他发现一个衣着光鲜的人在烟店里点雪茄烟，点烟的火晃来晃去。他的一把丝绸伞进门时放在门边了。索彼走进店，拿起伞，慢吞吞地走开。点雪茄烟的人忙赶过来。

"是我的伞！"他厉声道。

"这会是你的？"索彼用挖苦的声气反问，拿

① enchantment
/ɪnˈtʃɑːntmənt/ n. 魔法

② gibberish /ˈgɪbərɪʃ/ n. 胡言乱语，无意义的声音

③ twirl /twɜːl/ v. 使快速旋转

④ unattainable /ˌʌnəˈteɪnəbl/ a. 达不到的

⑤ petit /ˈpetiː/ a. 没有价值的，无用的，细小的
⑥ larceny /ˈlɑːsəni/ n. 盗窃（罪）

Why don't you call a cop? There stands one on the corner."

The umbrella owner slowed his steps. Soapy did likewise, with a presentiment that luck would again run against him. The policeman looked at the two curiously.

"Of course," said the umbrella man — "that is — well, you know how these mistakes occur — I — if it's your umbrella I hope you'll excuse me — I picked it up this morning in a restaurant — If you recognise it as yours, why — I hope you'll —"

Of course it's mine," said Soapy, **viciously**①."

The ex-umbrella man retreated. The policeman hurried to assist a tall blonde in an opera cloak across the street in front of a street car that was approaching two blocks away.

Soapy walked eastward through a street damaged by improvements. He hurled the umbrella wrathfully into an **excavation**②. He muttered against the men who wear helmets and carry clubs. Because he wanted to fall into their clutches, they seemed to regard him as a king who could do no wrong.

At length Soapy reached one of the avenues to the east where the **glitter**③ and **turmoil**④ was but faint. He set his face down this toward Madison Square, for the homing instinct survives even when the home is a park bench.

But on an unusually quiet corner Soapy came to a standstill. Here was an old church, **quaint**⑤ and **rambling**⑥ and **gabled**⑦. Through one violet-stained window a soft light glowed, where, no doubt, the organist loitered over the keys, making sure of his mastery of the coming Sabbath anthem. For there drifted out to Soapy's ears sweet music that caught and held him **transfixed**⑧ against the **convolutions**⑨ of the iron fence.

The moon was above, **lustrous**⑩ and serene; vehicles and pedestr-

了人家东西不说，还出言不逊。"那你干吗不叫警察呀？我就要拿。是你的伞呐！干吗不叫警察呀？街口就站着一个！"

伞的主人放慢了脚步。索彼也放慢脚步，心头有种不祥之感，觉得命运又会与他作对。警察看着他们俩，好生纳闷。

伞主人说："当——当然，唔——唔，你知道这种误会是怎么回事，就是我——要真是你的伞得请你原谅——我今天上午在餐馆捡到的。现在你认出来了，那——那还请你——"

"当然是我的伞！"索彼恶声恶气说。

伞的前主人收兵回营。警察呢，发现一位披着在剧场看戏穿的大外套的高个金发女郎在横过马路，又见两个街口外一辆电车正开来，便赶去帮那女的一把。

索彼往东走到一条在翻修的马路。他气得把伞扔进一个坑里，还咒骂那些戴头盔拿棍子的家伙。他有心让他们来抓，可是他们把他当成不可能有过失的圣贤。

最后索彼到了东西向一条没那么明亮和热闹的马路。他打定主意顺这条路回麦迪逊广场，因为他回家的天性并未泯灭，尽管他的家只是广场的一条长凳。

然而，在一个特别幽静的街口索彼站住了。这里有一座山形墙老教堂，虽不规整，却古色古香。一扇紫罗兰色的窗里还亮着灯，有位琴师反反复复练着琴，当然是为了在安息日唱圣歌时把琴弹得格外出色。索彼被飘来的优美音乐迷住了，靠在铁栏的圆环上出神。

天空挂着轮皎洁的明月，车辆与行人寥寥无

① viciously /'vɪʃəslɪ/ ad. 邪恶地,敌意地

② excavation /ˌekskə'veɪʃən/ n. 洞,穴,坑道

③ glitter /'glɪtə/ n. 闪光,闪耀

④ turmoil /'tɜːmɔɪl/ n. 骚动,混乱

⑤ quaint /kweɪnt/ a. 古雅的,奇特而有趣的

⑥ rambling /'ræmblɪŋ/ a. 漫步的,闲聊的

⑦ gabled /'geɪbld/ a. 有山墙的

⑧ transfix /træns'fɪks/ v. 刺穿,戳穿

⑨ convolution /ˌkɒnvə'luːʃən/ n. 卷积;旋转;圈,匝

⑩ lustrous /'lʌstrəs/ a. 有光泽的,光亮的

ians were few; sparrows twittered sleepily in the eaves — for a little while the scene might have been a country churchyard. And the anthem that the organist played cemented Soapy to the iron fence, for he had known it well in the days when his life contained such things as mothers and roses and ambitions and friends and **immaculate**① thoughts and collars.

The conjunction of Soapy's receptive state of mind and the influences about the old church wrought a sudden and wonderful change in his soul. He viewed with swift horror the pit into which he had tumbled, the degraded days, unworthy desires, dead hopes, wrecked **faculties**② and base motives that made up his existence.

And also in a moment his heart responded thrillingly to this novel mood. An instantaneous and strong impulse moved him to battle with his desperate fate. He would pull himself out of the **mire**③; he would make a man of himself again; he would conquer the evil that had taken possession of him. There was time; he was comparatively young yet; he would **resurrect** ④ his old eager ambitions and pursue them without **faltering**⑤. Those solemn but sweet organ notes had set up a revolution in him. To-morrow he would go into the roaring downtown district and find work. A fur importer had once offered him a place as driver. He would find him to-morrow and ask for the position. He would be somebody in the world. He would —

Soapy felt a hand laid on his arm. He looked quickly around into the broad face of a policeman.

"What are you doin' here? " asked the officer.

"Nothin'," said Soapy.

"Then come along," said the policeman.

"Three months on the Island," said the Magistrate in the Police Court the next morning.

儿，屋檐下的麻雀带着睡意叽叽喳喳叫了几声，眼下的景象会使人想起乡间教堂的墓地。琴师弹奏的圣歌把索彼牢牢拴在铁栏上了。以往他也曾享受过亲情、爱情，有过朋友，产生过抱负，思想洁白无瑕①，衣服干干净净，在那些日子他对圣歌非常熟悉。

索彼的心本就容易受感化，老教堂又有它的神力，所以，他的灵魂豁然醒悟。回想他跌进的深坑，回想那些不光彩的岁月，卑鄙的欲望，破灭的希望，毁弃的才能以及为谋生计而有过的肮脏动机，心头掠过一阵恐惧。

也是在一瞬间，经过这种反省后，他振作起来了。他感到一阵来得又快又猛的冲动，决心与坎坷的命运搏斗。他要从泥坑中自拔，要洗心革面，要战胜缠住了他的邪气。时间还来得及，他还相当年轻。他要重振往日的雄心，不屈不挠实现远大抱负。庄严而优美的琴声激起了他心灵深处的变化。明天他就去闹市区找工作。一位皮货进口商曾说愿雇他当司机。他明天去找他要这份工作。他会在世上有所作为的。他会……

索彼觉得有人抓住了他的手臂，忙一回头，看见了一个大脸盘的警察。

"你在这儿干什么？"警察问。

"没干什么。"索彼说。

"跟我走。"警察说。

第二天上午，警庭的法官宣布道："在岛上关押三个月。"

① immaculate /ɪˈmækjʊlɪt/ a. 洁净的，无污垢的

② faculty /ˈfækəltɪ/ n. 机能，官能

③ mire /maɪə/ n. 泥潭，沼泽，泥沼

④ resurrect /ˌrezəˈrekt/ v. 使复活，使复苏

⑤ falter /ˈfɔːltə/ v. 踉跄，摇晃；衰弱

这是一个关于希望的故事。

情感细腻的人对四时交替的感受总是比较强烈，正如黛玉看到落花会喟叹红颜老去，无所依处；乔安西将自己的生命寄托于窗外的几片藤叶。

生命是脆弱的，尤其是在艰难的人生中，但因为有了人与人之间无私的关爱，生命才有了坚强的意义，最后一片藤叶才能永远屹立枝头。

The Last Leaf

In a little district west of Washington Square the streets have run crazy and broken themselves into small strips called "places." These "places" make strange angles and curves. One street crosses itself a time or two. An artist once discovered a valuable possibility in this street. Suppose a collector with a bill for paints, paper and canvas should, in **traversing**[①] this route, suddenly meet himself coming back, without a cent having been paid on account!

So, to quaint old Greenwich Village the art people soon came **prowling**[②], hunting for north windows and eighteenth-century gables and Dutch attics and low rents. Then they imported some pewter mugs and a chafing dish or two from Sixth avenue, and became a "colony."

At the top of a squatty, three-story brick Sue and Johnsy had their studio. "Johnsy" was familiar for Joanna. One was from Maine; the other from California. They had met at the table d'hote of an Eighth street "Delmonico's," and found their tastes in art, **chicory**[③] salad and bishop sleeves so congenial that the joint studio resulted.

That was in May. In November a cold, unseen stranger, whom the doctors called **Pneumonia**[④], stalked about the colony, touching one here

最后一片叶

华盛顿广场往西有一小片地区的街道横七竖八，像乱摊着的小布条，名曰"胡同区"。这些胡同拐弯抹角，叫人摸不着头脑，甚至一条胡同会自身交叉一两回。有一次，一位画家发现，这种小巷也有一种难能可贵之处。要是有谁上这儿来收颜料、纸张、画布钱，说不定会沿街转回老地方，正好碰上一分一文都没收着的自己！

难怪，没多久那些搞艺术的人便纷至沓来，云集又古又怪的格林尼治村。他们图房租便宜，专找窗户朝北的房间、十八世纪山形墙屋和荷兰式小阁楼。又从第六大道买来几只大圆筒形锡杯，一两只火锅，建起了"殖民地"。

休伊与乔安西两人的画室就是在一栋矮墩墩的三层砖房的顶层。乔安西昵称为乔安娜。两人一个是缅因州人，一个是加利福尼亚州人，首次相逢是在第八街德尔蒙尼克饭店的餐桌上。她们同样爱好艺术，同样吃着凉拌菊苣，同样穿着大袖管衣服，两人一拍即合，便合租了一间房作画

① traverse /'trævɜːs/ v. 横越,横过

② prowl /praʊl/ v.（仔细地）搜寻;徘徊

③ chicory /'tʃɪkərɪ/ n. 菊苣

④ pneumonia /njuːˈməʊnjə/ n. 肺炎

and there with his icy fingers. Over on the east side this ravager strode boldly, **smiting**[1] his victims by scores, but his feet trod slowly through the maze of the narrow and moss-grown "places."

Mr. Pneumonia was not what you would call a **chivalric**[2] old gentleman. A mite of a little woman with blood thinned by California **zephyrs**[3] was hardly fair game for the red-fisted, short-breathed old duffer. But Johnsy he smote; and she lay, scarcely moving, on her painted iron bedstead, looking through the small Dutch window-panes at the blank side of the next brick house.

One morning the busy doctor invited Sue into the hallway with a **shaggy**[4], gray eyebrow.

"She has one chance in — let us say, ten," he said, as he shook down the mercury in his clinical **thermometer**[5]. "And that chance is for her to want to live. This way people have of lining-up on the side of the undertaker makes the entire **pharmacopeia**[6] look silly. Your little lady has made up her mind that she's not going to get well. Has she anything on her mind? "

"She — she wanted to paint the Bay of Naples some day," said Sue.

"Paint? — bosh! Has she anything on her mind worth thinking about twice — a man, for instance? "

"A man? " said Sue, with a jew's-harp twang in her voice. "Is a man worth — but, no, doctor; there is nothing of the kind."

"Well, it is the weakness, then," said the doctor. "I will do all that science, so far as it may **filter**[7] through my efforts, can accomplish. But whenever my patient begins to count the carriages in her funeral procession I subtract 50 per cent from the curative power of medicines. If you will get her to ask one question about the new winter styles in

① smite /smaɪt/ v. 重击，猛打

② chivalric /'ʃɪvəlrɪk/ a. 骑士时代的；侠义的

③ zephyr /'zefə/ n. 和风

④ shaggy /'ʃægɪ/ a. 有粗毛的

⑤ thermometer /θə'mɔmɪtə/ n. 温度计

⑥ pharmacop(o)eia /ˌfɑːməkə'piːə/ n. 药典

⑦ filter /'fɪltə/ v. 渗透

室。这是五月间的事。

到了十一月，一位冷心肠、看不见的不速之客闯进了这一带，伸出只冰凉的手今天碰碰这个，明天碰碰那个。医生称这位客人为"肺炎"。在广场以东，这瘟神简直横行无忌，害起人来一动手就几十，但走到长着青苔、迷宫似的"胡同区"，他放慢了脚步。

你绝不会说肺炎先生是位老侠士。让加利福尼亚州的和风都吹得没有了血色的弱女子哪会经得起喘粗气的老糊涂的铁拳？而他偏偏就打了乔安西。乔安西躺在油漆铁床上没有力气动弹，两眼呆望着荷兰式小窗对面的砖墙。

一天上午，那位忙碌的医生皱皱灰色浓眉，把休伊叫到过道里。

"现在十成希望只剩下一成。"医生一边甩下体温表里的水银一边说，"这成希望取决于她抱不抱活下去的决心。遇上一心想照顾棺材店生意的人，纵有灵丹妙药也不顶用。这位小姐已经认定自己再也好不了了。就不知她还有什么心事吗？"

"她——她希望有一天能去画那不勒斯湾。"休伊答道。

"画画？你扯到哪儿去啦！我是问她心里有没有还留恋的事。比方说，心里还会想着哪个男人。"

"男人？男人还会值得她想？"休伊的声音尖得像单簧口琴，"没这种事，大夫。"

"那就麻烦了。"医生说，"我一定尽力而为，凡医学上有的办法都会采用。但是如果病人盘算起会有多少辆马车来送葬，药物的疗效就要打个对折。要是她能问起今年冬天大衣的衣袖时兴什

cloak sleeves I will promise you a one-in-five chance for her, instead of one in ten."

After the doctor had gone Sue went into the workroom and cried a Japanese napkin to a pulp. Then she swaggered into Johnsy's room with her drawing board, whistling **ragtime**①.

Johnsy lay, scarcely making a **ripple**② under the bedclothes, with her face toward the window. Sue stopped whistling, thinking she was asleep.

She arranged her board and began a pen-and-ink drawing to illustrate a magazine story. Young artists must pave their way to Art by drawing pictures for magazine stories that young authors write to pave their way to Literature.

As Sue was sketching a pair of elegant horseshow riding trousers and a **monocle**③ on the figure of the hero, an **Idaho**④ cowboy, she heard a low sound, several times repeated. She went quickly to the bedside.

Johnsy's eyes were open wide. She was looking out the window and counting — counting backward.

"Twelve," she said, and a little later "eleven;" and then "ten," and "nine;" and then "eight" and "seven," almost together.

Sue looked **solicitously**⑤ out the window. What was there to count? There was only a bare, **dreary**⑥ yard to be seen, and the blank side of the brick house twenty feet, away. An old, old ivy vine, **gnarled**⑦ and decayed at the roots, climbed half way up the brick wall. The cold breath of autumn had stricken its leaves from the vine until its **skeleton**⑧ branches clung, almost bare, to the crumbling bricks.

"What is it, dear? " asked Sue.

"Six," said Johnsy, in almost a whisper. "They're falling faster now. Three days ago there were almost a hundred. It made my head ache

么式样，那么我对你说吧，她的希望就不是一成，
而是两成。"

医生走了以后，休伊到画室里哭了一场，把
条日本餐巾哭得透湿。哭过后她拿着画板昂首阔
步走进乔安西的房间，还一边吹口哨，吹音律多
的切分音。

乔安西脸朝窗躺在被窝里，一动没动。休伊
以为她睡着了，忙不吹了。

她摆好画板，开始替杂志社作小说的钢笔画
插图。年轻作者要踏上文学之路得先替杂志社写
短篇小说，美术工作者要闯出艺术之路得先替杂
志社作小说的插图。

小说的主人公是爱达荷州的牛仔，休伊在画
主人公穿的漂亮马裤和单眼镜时，好几次听到一
个微弱的声音。她赶紧走到床边。

乔安西睁大着眼在望着窗外边数数，是倒着
数的。

"十二，"她数着。过了一会儿，"十一。"又
过了会儿，"十，""九。"又过了会儿，"八，"
"七。"两个数几乎是接着数。

休伊觉得奇怪，看着窗外。有什么可数呢？
见到的只是个空荡荡的冷落院子和二十英尺外一
栋砖房的墙。一根老而又老的藤扒在墙上，有半
堵墙高，巴巴结结，靠近根部的地方已经萎缩，
藤叶几乎全被冷飕飕的秋风吹落，只剩下光秃秃
的枝干还紧贴在破败的墙上。

"怎么啦？"休伊问。

"六，"乔安西又在数，声音低得几乎听不见，
"现在落得快了。三天前还有将近一百，叫我数得

① ragtime /'rægtaɪm/ n. 繁
音拍子（多切分节奏的一
种早期爵士乐）
② ripple /'rɪpl/ n. 涟漪，细
浪，波纹

③ monocle /'mɒnəkl/ n. 单
片眼镜
④ Idaho /'aɪdəhəu/ n. 美国
爱达荷州

⑤ solicitously /sə'lɪsɪtəslɪ/
ad. 热心地，热切地
⑥ dreary /'drɪərɪ/ a. 沉闷的，
阴郁的
⑦ gnarled /nɑːld/ a. (树)多瘤
的，多节的
⑧ skeleton /'skelɪtn/ n. 骨骼，
骸骨

to count them. But now it's easy. There goes another one. There are only five left now."

"Five what, dear. Tell your Sudie."

"Leaves. On the ivy vine. When the last one falls I must go, too. I've known that for three days. Didn't the doctor tell you? "

"Oh, I never heard of such nonsense," complained Sue, with magnificent scorn. "What have old ivy leaves to do with your getting well? And you used to love that vine so, you naughty girl. Don't be a **goosey**[①]. Why, the doctor told me this morning that your chances for getting well real soon were — let's see exactly what he said — he said the chances were ten to one! Why, that's almost as good a chance as we have in New York when we ride on the street cars or walk past a new building. Try to take some broth now, and let Sudie go back to her drawing, so she can sell the editor man with it, and buy port wine for her sick child, and pork chops for her greedy self."

"You needn't get any more wine," said Johnsy, keeping her eyes fixed out the window. "There goes another. No, I don't want any broth. That leaves just four. I want to see the last one fall before it gets dark. Then I'll go, too."

"Johnsy, dear," said Sue, bending over her, "will you promise me to keep your eyes closed, and not look out the window until I am done working? I must hand those drawings in by to-morrow. I need the light, or I would draw the shade down."

"Couldn't you draw in the other room?" asked Johnsy, coldly.

"I'd rather be here by you," said Sue. "Besides I don't want you to keep looking at those silly ivy leaves."

"Tell me as soon as you have finished," said Johnsy, closing her eyes, and lying white and still as a fallen statue, "because I want to see

头发痛。现在容易。又掉了一片，只剩下五片。"

"五片什么？快跟我说。"

"五片藤叶。那根藤上的。等最后一片掉下来，我也就完了。早三天我已经明白。难道医生没对你说？"

"嘿，我才不听那种胡话。"休伊觉得这太荒唐，不屑一顾地说，"一根老藤上的叶子跟你的病好不好得了有什么相干！你以前多喜欢那根藤！丫头，别胡闹。你分明是犯傻。今天上午医生还对我说，你很快好起来的希望是——让我想想他的原话——对啦，他说你的希望有九成！想想看，这可以比作我们到了纽约，不管坐电车还是走路，十有八九能路过一栋新房子。来，喝点儿汤，喝了我就再画画，卖给编辑，得了钱给你这病娃娃买名牌红葡萄酒，再买点猪排，给我自己解馋。"

"葡萄酒用不着再买，"乔安西说，眼睛还盯着窗外，"又掉了一片。汤我也不要。只剩下四片叶了。要是天黑前我看到最后一片掉下来就好，见到了我也好闭眼。"

"乔安西，你听我的，闭上眼睛，别再看窗外，等我把这幅插图画完，怎么样？"休伊弯下身对她说，"这些画明天等着交。画画光线得好，要不然，我就会把窗帘放下。"

"那你不能到别的房间画？"乔安西没好气地反问。

"我得在这儿陪着你。再说，我也不能让你看着几片藤叶发傻气。"休伊答道。

"那你画完了得告诉我，我想看着最后一片飘

① goosey /'guːsɪ/ n. 呆子

the last one fall. I'm tired of waiting. I'm tired of thinking. I went to turn loose my hold on everything, and go sailing down, down, just like one of those poor, tired leaves."

"Try to sleep," said Sue. "I must call Behrman up to be my model for the old hermit miner. I'll not be gone a minute. Don't try to move 'till I come back."

Old Behrman was a painter who lived on the ground floor beneath them. He was past sixty and had a Michael Angelo's Moses beard curling down from the head of a satyr along the body of an imp. Behrman was a failure in art. Forty years he had **wielded**[1] the brush without getting near enough to touch the hem of his Mistress's robe. He had been always about to paint a **masterpiece**[2], but had never yet begun it. For several years he had painted nothing except now and then a daub in the line of commerce or advertising. He earned a little by serving as a model to those young artists in the colony who could not pay the price of a professional. He drank gin to excess, and still talked of his coming masterpiece. For the rest he was a fierce little old man, who **scoffed**[3] terribly at softness in any one, and who regarded himself as especial mastiff-in-waiting to protect the two young artists in the studio above.

Sue found Behrman smelling strongly of juniper berries in his **dimly**[4] lighted den below. In one corner was a blank canvas on an **easel**[5] that had been waiting there for twenty-five years to receive the first line of the masterpiece. She told him of Johnsy's fancy, and how she feared she would, indeed, light and fragile as a leaf herself, float away when her slight hold upon the world grew weaker.

Old Behrman, with his red eyes, plainly streaming, shouted his contempt and **derision**[6] for such idiotic imaginings.

下来。"乔安西边说边闭上眼睛，脸惨白，躺着不动，像尊倒下的石膏像，"我不愿再等。也不愿想什么。一切我都不要了，只愿像一片没有了生命力的败叶一样，往下飘，飘。"

"安心睡一会儿吧，"休伊说，"我画退隐的老矿工要个模特儿，得找贝尔曼来。我只出去一会儿。别动，等我回来。"

贝尔曼老头也能画画，就住在下面一楼。他已年过六旬，头像希腊神话中半人半兽的森林神的，身子像小鬼的，胡须像米开朗琪罗的摩西雕像的，鬈曲着从头顺身子往下垂。他作画没搞出个名堂来，挥舞了四十年的画笔，却连艺术女神的长衫边都没碰着。他一心要画出个惊人之作，但至今还没开笔。近些年除了涂涂抹抹弄一张商业画或广告画，他什么也没搞，就靠替这一带请不起职业模特儿的年轻画家当模特儿挣几个钱。他喝起杜松子酒来没有节制，还不停叨念要搞的惊人之作。此外这小个子老头还像个凶神恶煞，谁软绵绵的就瞧不起谁，自诩为保护楼上两位年轻画家的看家猛犬。

休伊去时贝尔曼果然在楼下他那间又暗又邋遢的房间里，浑身杜松子酒气冲天。屋角里画架上绷着块白画布，就等画上幅惊人之作，但等了二十五年还是一笔未画。休伊告诉他，乔安西在胡思乱想，把自己比作一片弱不禁风的藤叶，等到力气亏空，在这世界再也扒不住时，会飘落下来。

贝尔曼老头的一双红眼睛正不停地流泪，但听到这般白痴似的胡想，他连鄙薄带挖苦地叫了一阵。

① wield /wiːld/ v. 挥舞（剑等），使用（工具等）
② masterpiece /'mɑːstəpiːs/ n. 杰作，名作
③ scoff /skɒf/ v. 嘲笑，嘲弄
④ dimly /'dɪmlɪ/ ad. 昏暗地；朦胧地
⑤ easel /'iːzl/ n. 画架，黑板架
⑥ derision /dɪ'rɪʒən/ n. 嘲笑，嘲弄

"Vass!" he cried. "Is dere people in de world mit der foolishness to die because leafs dey drop off from a confounded vine? I haf not heard of such a thing. No, I will not bose as a model for your fool hermit-dunderhead. Vy do you allow dot silly pusiness to come in der prain of her? Ach, dot poor lettle Miss Johnsy."

"She is very ill and weak," said Sue, "and the fever has left her mind **morbid**① and full of strange fancies. Very well, Mr. Behrman, if you do not care to pose for me, you needn't. But I think you are a horrid old — old **flibbertigibbet**②."

"You are just like a woman!" yelled Behrman. "Who said I will not bose? Go on. I come mit you. For half an hour I haf peen trying to say dot I am ready to bose. Gott! dis is not any blace in which one so goot as Miss Yohnsy shall lie sick. Some day I vill baint a masterpiece, and ve shall all go away. Gott! yes."

Johnsy was sleeping when they went upstairs. Sue pulled the shade down to the window-sill, and motioned Behrman into the other room. In there they peered out the window fearfully at the ivy vine. Then they looked at each other for a moment without speaking. A persistent, cold rain was falling, mingled with snow. Behrman, in his old blue shirt, took his seat as the hermit-miner on an upturned kettle for a rock.

When Sue awoke from an hour's sleep the next morning she found Johnsy with dull, wide-open eyes staring at the drawn green shade.

"Pull it up; I want to see," she ordered, in a whisper.

Wearily Sue obeyed.

But, lo! after the beating rain and fierce gusts of wind that had endured through the livelong night, there yet stood out against the brick wall one ivy leaf. It was the last on the vine. Still dark green near its

"什么话！"他嚷着，"看到混账藤叶子掉了就会想死，阳世上还真有这种蠢货？这种事还是头一回听说。叫我陪你们胡闹，当什么退隐的笨驴的模特儿，我可不爱干。你怎么让那种娘们儿的胡思乱想钻到她脑瓜子里去啦？哎哟，乔安西那小家伙也可怜。"

"她病得厉害，身体太虚弱。"休伊说，"脑子烧糊涂了，老胡思乱想。贝尔曼先生，既然你不愿给我当模特儿，那就算了，没关系。不过我看，你这老头也够呛，太啰唆。"

"你们女人就是女人！"贝尔曼又是大喊大叫起来，"谁说的我不干？走吧，我跟你去。我说了这老半天意思就是愿意干。天老爷！乔安西小姐是大好人，怎么就病倒在这种地方？哪天我画出张绝妙的画儿，我们一块儿远走高飞。老天爷！行啦。"

两人上楼时乔安西睡着了。休伊把窗帘放到底，打个手势把贝尔曼带进了另一间房。他们在房里瞧着窗外的那根藤，心里不由得害怕。接着，两人你看我，我看你，好一会儿没说话。冰冷的雨在不停地下，还夹着雪。贝尔曼穿件旧蓝色衬衫，坐到个翻转的水壶上当退隐的矿工，那水壶是充作石头的。

休伊只睡了一个小时，到早上醒来时，只见乔安西睁大两只无神的眼睛盯住放了下来的绿窗帘。

"卷起来，我要看。"她有气无力说。

休伊照办了，也是有气无力。

可是，看啊！经过漫漫长夜的风吹雨打，竟然还有一片藤叶扒在砖墙上。这是藤上的最后一

① morbid /'mɔːbɪd/ a. 疾病的

② flibbertigibbet /'flɪbətɪ'dʒɪbɪt/ n. 饶舌的人

stem, but with its **serrated**[1] edges tinted with the yellow of **dissolution**[2] and decay, it hung bravely from a branch some twenty feet above the ground.

"It is the last one," said Johnsy. "I thought it would surely fall during the night. I heard the wind. It will fall to-day, and I shall die at the same time."

"Dear, dear!" said Sue, leaning her worn face down to the pillow, "think of me, if you won't think of yourself. What would I do?"

But Johnsy did not answer. The **lonesomest**[3] thing in all the world is a soul when it is making ready to go on its mysterious, far journey. The fancy seemed to possess her more strongly as one by one the ties that bound her to friendship and to earth were loosed.

The day wore away, and even through the twilight they could see the lone ivy leaf clinging to its stem against the wall. And then, with the coming of the night the north wind was again loosed, while the rain still beat against the windows and pattered down from the low Dutch eaves.

When it was light enough Johnsy, the **merciless**[4], commanded that the shade be raised.

The ivy leaf was still there.

Johnsy lay for a long time looking at it. And then she called to Sue, who was **stirring**[5] her chicken broth over the gas stove.

"I've been a bad girl, Sudie," said Johnsy. "Something has made that last leaf stay there to show me how wicked I was. It is a sin to want to die. You may bring me a little broth now, and some milk with a little port in it, and — no; bring me a hand-mirror first, and then pack some pillows about me, and I will sit up and watch you cook."

An hour later she said.

① serrate /'sereɪt/ a. 锯齿状
的,有锯齿的
② dissolution /ˌdɪsə'luːʃən/
n. 分解;溶解;融化

③ lonesome /'ləʊnsəm/ a. 寂
寞的,孤单的

④ merciless /'mɜːsɪlɪs/ a. 无
情的,残酷的

⑤ stir /stɜː/ v. 搅拌,搅动

片叶,叶柄附近依旧深绿,但锯齿形边缘已经枯败发黄。它顽强地挂在离地面二十英尺高的一根枝上。

"这是最后一片叶,"乔安西说,"我还以为晚上它准会掉。我听见了风声。今天它会掉的,我的死期也就来了。"

"乖乖,乖乖! 你不愿为自己着想也得为我着想。丢下我怎么办呢?"休伊说,把消瘦的脸贴到枕头上。

但是乔安西没有答话。即将踏上黄泉路的人的心灵是无比孤寂的。乔安西与朋友、与人世一步一步拉开了距离,而幻觉在这时间便越来越难摆脱。

这一天慢慢过去了,尽管天色已暗下来,她们还是能看见那片孤零零的藤叶牢牢扒在墙上。后来,夜幕降临,北风又紧,雨敲打着窗户,也从矮荷兰式屋檐上倾泻而下。

天刚亮,乔安西不管三七二十一就叫拉开窗帘。

藤叶还在。

乔安西躺在床上久久看着。后来她叫唤休伊,休伊正在翻动煤气炉上鸡汤里的鸡。

乔安西说:"休伊,我太不应该。不知是怎么鬼使神差的,那片叶老掉不下来,可见我原来犯了错。想死是罪过。你这就给我盛点鸡汤来,还有牛奶,牛奶里搁点葡萄酒——等等! 先拿面小镜子来,再把几个枕头垫到我身边,让我坐起来看你烧菜。"

过了一小时,她说:

"Sudie, some day I hope to paint the Bay of Naples."

The doctor came in the afternoon, and Sue had an excuse to go into the hallway as he left.

"Even chances," said the doctor, taking Sue's thin, shaking hand in his. "With good nursing you'll win. And now I must see another case I have downstairs. Behrman, his name is — some kind of an artist, I believe. Pneumonia, too. He is an old, weak man, and the attack is acute. There is no hope for him; but he goes to the hospital to-day to be made more comfortable."

The next day the doctor said to Sue: "She's out of danger. You've won. Nutrition and care now — that's all."

And that afternoon Sue came to the bed where Johnsy lay, contentedly **knitting** ① a very blue and very useless woolen shoulder scarf, and put one arm around her, pillows and all.

"I have something to tell you, white mouse," she said. "Mr. Behrman died of pneumonia to-day in the hospital. He was ill only two days. The **janitor**② found him on the morning of the first day in his room downstairs helpless with pain. His shoes and clothing were wet through and icy cold. They couldn't imagine where he had been on such a dreadful night. And then they found a lantern, still lighted, and a ladder that had been dragged from its place, and some scattered brushes, and a **palette**③ with green and yellow colors mixed on it, and — look out the window, dear, at the last ivy leaf on the wall. Didn't you wonder why it never fluttered or moved when the wind blew? Ah, darling, it's Behrman's masterpiece — he painted it there the night that the last leaf fell."

"休伊，我希望以后能去画那不勒斯湾。"

下午医生来了。医生刚走，休伊找个借口跑进走廊。

"有五成希望。"医生握着休易的手，说，"只要护理得好，就能战胜疾病。现在我得去楼下看另一个病人。他叫贝尔曼，也是个画画的。又是肺炎。他年纪大，体质弱，病又来势凶，已经没有了希望，但今天还是要送医院，医院的条件好些。"

第二天，医生对休伊说："她出了危险期。你们胜利了。剩下的事是营养和护理。"

这天下午，休伊坐到乔安西躺的床上，织着条根本用不着的蓝色羊毛披肩，已经无忧无虑。织着织着，她伸出只手连人带枕头搂着乔安西。

① knit /nɪt/ v. 编织

"有件事告诉你，小宝贝。"她说，"贝尔曼先生得肺炎今天死在医院。他只病了两天。头一天早上看门人在楼下房间发现他难受得要命，衣服、鞋子全湿了，摸起来冰凉。谁也猜不着他在又是风又是雨的夜晚上哪儿去了。后来他们发现了一盏灯笼，还亮着，又发现梯子搬动了地方，几支画笔东一支西一支扔着，一块调色板上调了绿颜料和黄颜料。现在你看窗外，乖乖。墙上还扒着最后一片藤叶。你不是奇怪为什么风吹着它也不飘不动吗？唉，亲爱的，那是贝尔曼的杰作。在最后一片叶子落下来的晚上，他在墙上画了一片。"

② janitor /'dʒænɪtə/ n. 门卫，看门人

③ palette /'pælɪt/ n. 调色板

这是一个宿命论的故事。

你一定曾像戴维一样，犹豫不决地站在三岔路口，权衡着究竟哪一条路能通向更好的结局。

然而，残酷的事实是，人生的开端和结局也许都是命中注定了的。性情如此，气质如此，无论选择哪条路，最终都只会导向同一个结局。就如同努力学夜莺歌唱的戴维，在每条路的尽头，等待他的，都是同一颗穿胸而过的子弹。

这就是他的命运吧。

Roads of Destiny

I go to seek on many roads
What is to be.
True heart and strong, with love to light —
Will they not bear me in the fight
To order, **shun**[1] *or wield or mold*
My Destiny?

Unpublished Poems of David Mignot.

The song was over. The words were David's; the **air**[2], one of the countryside. The company about the inn table **applauded**[3] heartily, for the young poet paid for the wine. Only the **notary**[4], M. Papineau, shook his head a little at the lines, for he was a man of books, and he had not drunk with the rest.

David went out into the village street, where the night air drove the wine vapor from his head. And then he remembered that he and Yvonne had quarrelled that day, and that he had resolved to leave his home that night to seek fame and honor in the great world outside.

"When my poems are on every man's tongue," he told himself, in

命运之路

走上许多条路，
我寻找着命运。
忠诚的心，力量，再加上爱，
它们能不能使我
指挥，逃脱，摆布或者改变
我的命运？

——引自戴维·米尼奥未发表的诗

① shun /ʃʌn/ v. 躲开，回避

歌唱完了。歌词出自戴维之手，曲调具有乡土气息。酒店的人满座热烈鼓掌，其原因是这位年轻诗人出了酒钱。只有公证人帕皮诺先生例外，听完歌摇了摇头。一来他是读书人，二来别人喝了酒他没喝。

② air /'eə/ n. 曲调，旋律
③ applaud /ə'plɔːd/ v. 鼓掌欢迎，喝彩
④ notary /'nəʊtərɪ/ n. 公证人，公证员

戴维出酒店走到小镇的街上被晚风一吹，把酒意吹醒了，这才想起白天和伊旺姑娘拌过嘴，他已下了决心当晚离开家，到外面的广阔世界去，定要闯个功成名就来。

"到我的诗脍炙人口的那一天，她也许会后悔今天气冲冲骂我。"想着想着，他觉得心里美

a fine **exhilaration**①, "she will, perhaps, think of the hard words she spoke this day."

Except the **roisterers**② in the tavern, the village folk were abed. David crept softly into his room in the shed of his father's cottage and made a bundle of his small store of clothing. With this upon a staff, he set his face outward upon the road that ran from Vernoy.

He passed his father's herd of sheep, **huddled**③ in their nightly pen — the sheep he **herded**④ daily, leaving them to **scatter**⑤ while he wrote verses on scraps of paper. He saw a light yet shining in Yvonne's window, and a weakness shook his purpose of a sudden. Perhaps that light meant that she **rued**⑥, sleepless, her anger, and that morning might — But, no! His decision was made. Vernoy was no place for him. Not one soul there could share his thoughts. Out along that road lay his fate and his future.

Three leagues across the dim, moonlit **champaign**⑦ ran the road, straight as a **ploughman**⑧'s furrow. It was believed in the village that the road ran to Paris, at least; and this name the poet whispered often to himself as he walked. Never so far from Vernoy had David travelled before.

THE LEFT BRANCH

Three leagues, then, the road ran, and turned into a puzzle. It joined with another and a larger road at right angles. David stood, uncertain, for a while, and then took the road to the left.

Upon this more important highway were, imprinted in the dust, wheel tracks left by the recent passage of some vehicle. Some half an hour later these traces were **verified**⑨ by the sight of a **ponderous**⑩

① exhilaration
/ɪgˌzɪləˈreɪʃən/ n. 愉快的
心情,高兴

② roisterer /ˈrɔɪstərə/ n. 闹
饮者,喧闹作乐者

③ huddle /ˈhʌdl/ v. 挤作一
团,聚在一起

④ herd /hɜːd/ v. 聚在一起,
成群

⑤ scatter /ˈskætə/ v. 分散,
溃散

⑥ rue /ruː/ v. 懊悔,后悔,悔
恨

⑦ champaign /ˈtræmpeɪn/ n.
平原,原野

⑧ ploughman /ˈplaʊmən/ n.
农夫,犁田者

⑨ verify /ˈverɪfaɪ/ v. 证明,
证实

⑩ ponderous /ˈpɒndərəs/ a. 沉
重的,笨重的

滋滋的。

　　除了酒店的一帮酒鬼,镇上的人都睡了。他轻手轻脚摸进他在父亲家的房间,把几件衣服打成小包,用根棍挑着,转身出门踏上离开弗洛伊之路。

　　他经过父亲的羊群,夜晚羊在栏里挤成了一堆。每天他要去放羊,可是他只顾在纸上写诗,听凭羊东一只西一只乱跑。看到伊旺的房里还亮着灯,突然他又犹豫了。也许,有灯就意味着她睡不着,后悔不该发火,到早上可能就……然而,不行!他的决心下定了。弗洛伊不是他的久留之地,这儿没一个人与他志同道合。沿着出镇的路走,他会交上好运,会前程远大。

　　路在月光下半明半暗的平原上延伸开来,长九英里,直得像用犁耕出来的,镇上的人都说至少直通巴黎,诗人一路走一路默默念了又念巴黎这两个字。戴维至今没到过离弗洛伊那么远的地方。

往左的路

　　走出九英里地,遇到了一个难题,到了一个岔路口。一条更宽的路与这条成直角相交。戴维站住犹豫了一会儿,然后上了左边的路。

　　这条大路上有几条刚过去不久的车留下的车轮印。果然,走了约半小时,只见一辆大马车陷进了一座陡峭的小山山脚下的小溪里。车夫和副手吆喝着在拽马缰。路边站着一男一女,男的身

carriage mired in a little brook at the bottom of a steep hill. The driver and postilions were shouting and tugging at the horses' bridles. On the road at one side stood a huge, black-clothed man and a **slender**[1] lady wrapped in a long, light cloak.

David saw the lack of skill in the efforts of the servants. He quietly assumed control of the work. He directed the **outriders**[2] to cease their clamor at the horses and to exercise their strength upon the wheels. The driver alone urged the animals with his familiar voice; David himself heaved a powerful shoulder at the rear of the carriage, and with one harmonious tug the great vehicle rolled up on solid ground. The outriders climbed to their places.

David stood for a moment upon one foot. The huge gentleman waved a hand. "You will enter the carriage," he said, in a voice large, like himself, but smoothed by art and habit. **Obedience**[3] belonged in the path of such a voice. Brief as was the young poet's hesitation, it was cut shorter still by a renewal of the command. David's foot went to the step. In the darkness he perceived dimly the form of the lady upon the rear seat. He was about to seat himself opposite, when the voice again swayed him to its will. "You will sit at the lady's side."

The gentleman swung his great weight to the forward seat. The carriage proceeded up the hill. The lady was shrunk, silent, into her corner. David could not estimate whether she was old or young, but a delicate, mild perfume from her clothes stirred his poet's fancy to the belief that there was loveliness beneath the mystery. Here was an adventure such as he had often imagined. But as yet he held no key to it, for no word was spoken while he sat with his **impenetrable**[4] companions.

In an hour's time David **perceived**[5] through the window that the

材魁伟，穿身黑衣，女的身材苗条，裹着件浅色长斗篷。

戴维看到几个仆人用力不得法，也不多说，就走过去教他们怎么干。他要副手别对着马大喊大叫，应使力气推车轮。马熟悉车夫的声音，吆喝马的只车夫一个就够了。戴维自己用强壮的肩膀在车后顶。齐心协力一使劲，大马车推上了坚硬的路面。副手跳上了原来的位置。

戴维单腿立地站了一会儿。"你坐到车里来，"身材魁伟的人一挥手说。他个子大，声音也大，但举止倒温文尔雅。这威严的声音让人唯有服从。年轻的诗人稍一犹豫，又听到了一声喊，顿时不再迟疑。戴维踩上了踏板。黑暗中他隐约看到车后坐着那女人。他正想往她的对面坐，谁知那声音又对他下了一道命令："你坐到这位小姐旁边。"

那男人沉重的身躯压到了前面座位上。马车开始上山。那女人在座位上缩成一团，也不出声。戴维判断不出她年老年少，只觉得她衣服里透出轻柔的香味，不禁动了诗人的想象力，认定这神秘中必包含了美妙。这情景正是他经常幻想的奇遇。然而现在他摸不清底细，因为与他同坐在车上的两位高深莫测的人物没开口说一句话。

过了一小时光景，戴维透过车窗看到车走到了一个市镇的街上。没多久，车停在一所关了门、灭了灯的房子前，一个副手下了车没好气地擂起

① slender /'slendə/ a. 修长的,苗条的,纤细的

② outrider /'aʊtˌraɪdə/ n. 骑乘侍从

③ obedience /ə'biːdjəns/ n. 服从,顺从

④ impenetrable /ɪm'penɪtrəbl/ a. 不能通过的,不能穿过的

⑤ perceive /pə'siːv/ v. 察觉,感知

vehicle traversed the street of some town. Then it stopped in front of a closed and darkened house, and a postilion alighted to hammer impatiently upon the door. A latticed window above flew wide and a nightcapped head popped out.

"Who are ye that disturb honest folk at this time of night? My house is closed. 'Tis too late for profitable travellers to be abroad. Cease knocking at my door, and be off."

"Open! " **spluttered**[1] the postilion, loudly; "open for Monsiegneur the **Marquis**[2] de Beaupertuys."

"Ah! " cried the voice above. "Ten thousand pardons, my lord. I did not know — the hour is so late — at once shall the door be opened, and the house placed at my lord's disposal."

Inside was heard the clink of chain and bar, and the door was flung open. Shivering with chill and **apprehension**[3], the landlord of the Silver Flagon stood, half clad, candle in hand, upon the **threshold**[4].

David followed the Marquis out of the carriage. "Assist the lady," he was ordered. The poet obeyed. He felt her small hand tremble as he guided her **descent**[5]. "Into the house," was the next command.

The room was the long dining-hall of the tavern. A great oak table ran down its length. The huge gentleman seated himself in a chair at the nearer end. The lady sank into another against the wall, with an air of great weariness. David stood, considering how best he might now take his leave and continue upon his way.

"My lord," said the landlord, bowing to the floor, "h-had I ex-expected this honor, entertainment would have been ready. T-t-there is wine and cold fowl and m-m-maybe — "

"Candles," said the marquis, spreading the fingers of one **plump**[6] white hand in a gesture he had.

门来。突然楼上一扇格子窗开了，伸出个戴睡帽的头。

"三更半夜的，是谁乱敲门？我这门不开！不分早晚往外审，有钱也没人要赚你的。快别打门啦，走吧。"

"开门！"副手使劲嚷嚷，"快开门，是博贝尔杜依侯爵老爷。"

"哎呀，我的天，恕罪，恕罪！"楼上的人叫道，"我不知道是——就怪天太晚。马上开门。这屋子随老爷怎么住都行。"

屋子里响起了解铁链下门闩的声音，大门马上洞开。银瓶旅社的店主手拿蜡烛站在门口，披着件衣，又发冷又害怕，直哆嗦。

戴维跟着侯爵下了车。一道命令下了来："扶小姐一把。"诗人遵了命。他觉得扶小姐下车时，她的小手在颤抖着。接着又是一道命令："进来！"

他们进了店里的长餐厅。一张大梓木桌竖摆着，和餐厅一样长。身材魁伟的侯爵坐到下首的一张椅上，那小姐倒在靠墙的一张椅上，看来已精疲力竭。戴维站着，考虑该怎样告辞继续赶路才好。

"老爷，要是早知道您大驾光临，在下一定会早早准备。"店主人说，一个深鞠躬都碰了地，"现在只有酒，冷鸡，也——也许……"

"蜡烛！"侯爵一只又白又胖的手指头一张，做了个他特有的手势。

① splutter /'splʌtə/ v. 气急败坏地说话
② marquis /'mɑːkwɪs/ n. 侯爵
③ apprehension /ˌæprɪ'henʃən/ n. 恐惧，忧虑
④ threshold /'θreʃhəʊld/ n. 门槛
⑤ descent /dɪ'sent/ n. 下来，下去
⑥ plump /plʌmp/ a. 丰满的，胖嘟嘟的

"Y-yes, my lord." He fetched half a dozen candles, lighted them, and set them upon the table.

"If **monsieur**① would, perhaps, deign to taste a certain Burgundy — there is a cask — "

"Candles," said monsieur, spreading his fingers.

"Assuredly — quickly — I fly, my lord."

A dozen more lighted candles shone in the hall. The great bulk of the marquis overflowed his chair. He was dressed in fine black from head to foot save for the snowy **ruffles**② at his wrist and throat. Even the hilt and **scabbard**③ of his sword were black. His expression was one of **sneering**④ pride. The ends of an upturned moustache reached nearly to his mocking eyes.

The lady sat motionless, and now David perceived that she was young, and possessed of pathetic and appealing beauty. He was startled from the **contemplation**⑤ of her **forlorn**⑥ loveliness by the booming voice of the marquis.

"What is your name and pursuit? "

"David Mignot. I am a poet."

The moustache of the marquis curled nearer to his eyes.

"How do you live? "

"I am also a **shepherd**⑦; I guarded my father's flock," David answered, with his head high, but a flush upon his cheek.

"Then listen, master shepherd and poet, to the fortune you have **blundered upon**⑧ to-night. This lady is my niece, **Mademoiselle**⑨ Lucie de Varennes. She is of noble descent and is possessed of ten thousand francs a year in her own right. As to her charms, you have but to observe for yourself. If the inventory pleases your shepherd's heart, she becomes your wife at a word. Do not interrupt me. To-night I conveyed

① monsieur /mə'sjɜː/ n.（法语）先生

"是，老爷！"店主人拿来六根蜡烛，点着了摆在桌上。

"如果侯爵大人赏光喝——喝勃艮地，那——那一桶……"

"蜡烛！"侯爵说，又叉开了指头。

"遵命！我这就——快——快拿——老爷。"

又点了十二根，照得房间通亮。侯爵坐的靠椅还容不下他的大身躯。他上下一身漂亮的黑衣裤，只有袖口和领口的褶边是雪白的。他佩剑的剑鞘与剑柄也是黑色。满脸瞧不起人的高傲神气。八字胡高高翘起，两端几乎碰着了傲气十足的眼睛。

② ruffle /'rʌfl/ n. 褶裥饰边
③ scabbard /'skæbəd/ n. 鞘

④ sneer /snɪə/ v. 轻蔑地笑，冷笑

那小姐坐着一动没动，这时戴维才看出她年纪很轻，有着摄人心魄的美貌。他正望着她凄美的神态出神时，侯爵的大嗓门把他惊醒了。

⑤ contemplation
/ˌkɒntem ' pleɪʃən/ n. 凝视；沉思，冥想
⑥ forlorn /fə'lɔːn/ a. 被遗弃的，孤独的

"你叫什么名字？是干什么的？"

"戴维·米尼奥。我是个诗人。"

侯爵的八字胡翘得离眼睛更近了。

"你靠什么过活？"

"我还放羊，替我父亲看羊。"戴维答话时高昂着头，可是脸上泛起了羞色。

⑦ shepherd /'ʃepəd/ n. 牧羊人，羊倌

"好吧，羊倌诗人，你听听今天晚上阴差阳错你交了什么运。这位小姐是我的侄女，叫露西·瓦伦小姐。她出身显贵，名下一年有一万法郎收入。至于她的美貌，你自己看看就知道了。如果这一大堆好处能称你羊倌的心，只消一句话她就可以做你的老婆。请你没听完别岔断我的话。今天晚上我送她去维尔莫伯爵的城堡，因为她早已许配

⑧ blunder upon 偶然碰上，无意中发现
⑨ mademoiselle
/ˌmædəmwə'zel/ n.（法语）小姐（对未婚女子的尊称）

her to the **chateau**^① of the Comte de Villemaur, to whom her hand had been promised. Guests were present; the priest was waiting; her marriage to one **eligible** ^② in rank and fortune was ready to be accomplished. At the altar this **demoiselle**^③, so meek and dutiful, turned upon me like a leopardess, charged me with cruelty and crimes, and broke, before the gaping priest, the **troth**^④ I had **plighted**^⑤ for her. I swore there and then, by ten thousand devils, that she should marry the first man we met after leaving the chateau, be he prince, charcoal-burner, or thief. You, shepherd, are the first. Mademoiselle must be wed this night. If not you, then another. You have ten minutes in which to make your decision. Do not vex me with words or questions. Ten minutes, shepherd; and they are speeding."

The marquis drummed loudly with his white fingers upon the table. He sank into a veiled attitude of waiting. It was as if some great house had shut its doors and windows against approach. David would have spoken, but the huge man's bearing stopped his tongue. Instead, he stood by the lady's chair and bowed.

"Mademoiselle," he said, and he **marvelled**^⑥ to find his words flowing easily before so much elegance and beauty. "You have heard me say I was a shepherd. I have also had the fancy, at times, that I am a poet. If it be the test of a poet to adore and cherish the beautiful, that fancy is now strengthened. Can I serve you in any way, mademoiselle? "

The young woman looked up at him with eyes dry and mournful. His frank, glowing face, made serious by the **gravity**^⑦ of the adventure, his strong, straight figure and the liquid sympathy in his blue eyes, perhaps, also, her **imminent**^⑧ need of long-denied help and kindness, thawed her to sudden tears.

① chateau /ˈʃɑːtəʊ/ n.（法国的）城堡，酒庄

② eligible /ˈelɪdʒəbl/ a. 有资格当选的

③ demoiselle /ˌdemwɑːˈzel/ n.（法语）少女

④ troth /trəʊθ/ n. 订婚

⑤ plight /plaɪt/ v. 盟誓

⑥ marvel /ˈmɑːvəl/ v. 感到惊讶

⑦ gravity /ˈɡrævɪtɪ/ n. 重要性

⑧ imminent /ˈɪmɪnənt/ a. 临近的，即将发生的，逼近的

给那伯爵。宾客已经到齐，神父也在等着，她本要与一位又有钱又有地位的人完婚。到了圣坛前，这位温柔听话的小姐突然像一头母豹一样向我扑来，骂我冷酷无情，作恶多端，把我为她订的婚事毁了，弄得牧师目瞪口呆。我当场指天地发誓，要在离开城堡后把她嫁给我们遇上的第一个人，无论这个人是王子也罢，烧炭工也罢，贼也罢。羊倌，你就是我们遇上的第一个人。今天晚上这位小姐非嫁不可。如果你不愿，那就嫁给下一个。你考虑十分钟后作决定。你别对我说话烦我，也别问这问那。羊倌，十分钟，这就开始了。"

侯爵用白皙的手指把桌子敲得咚咚响。然后他不动声色地等待着，似乎把一座大厦的门窗全关闭了，谁也不让进。戴维本想说话，但这位大个子的神态使他开不了口。他转而站到千金小姐坐的椅子边，鞠了一躬。

"小姐，你已经听我说了我原来放过羊。可是我也常想，我是位诗人。"戴维说道，心里却暗自奇怪，不知为什么在这位温文尔雅的大美人前会话如泉涌，"有人说检验诗人要看他是否爱美、惜美，现在看来，果然如此。小姐，我怎样才能为你效劳呢？"

年轻姑娘抬头看着他，眼里没有泪水，只有悲伤。他的脸显得坦率，热情，同时又因意外遇见一桩大事而庄重严肃；他的体格结实，身板笔挺；他的蓝眼睛闪着同情的泪光；也许是在这紧急关头，终于盼来了久违的善意和援手，姑娘终于也按捺不住夺眶而出的热泪。

"Monsieur," she said, in low tones, "you look to be true and kind. He is my uncle, the brother of my father, and my only relative. He loved my mother, and he hates me because I am like her. He has made my life one long terror. I am afraid of his very looks, and never before dared to disobey him. But to-night he would have married me to a man three times my age. You will forgive me for bringing this **vexation**[①] upon you, monsieur. You will, of course, decline this mad act he tries to force upon you. But let me thank you for your generous words, at least. I have had none spoken to me in so long."

There was now something more than generosity in the poet's eyes. Poet he must have been, for Yvonne was forgotten; this fine, new loveliness held him with its freshness and grace. The subtle perfume from her filled him with strange emotions. His tender look fell warmly upon her. She leaned to it, thirstily.

"Ten minutes," said David, "is given me in which to do what I would devote years to achieve. I will not say I pity you, mademoiselle; it would not be true — I love you. I cannot ask love from you yet, but let me rescue you from this cruel man, and, in time, love may come. I think I have a future; I will not always be a shepherd. For the present I will cherish you with all my heart and make your life less sad. Will you trust your fate to me, mademoiselle? "

"Ah, you would sacrifice yourself from pity! "

"From love. The time is almost up, mademoiselle."

"You will regret it, and despise me."

"I will live only to make you happy, and myself worthy of you."

Her fine small hand crept into his from beneath her cloak.

"I will trust you," she breathed, "with my life. And — and love —

"先生，"她用低低的声音说，"我看得出你是个诚实善良的人。这个人是我的叔父，也是我唯一的亲戚。他原来爱过我母亲，现在恨我是因为我像母亲。他一直使我在恐惧中过日子。我见到他就害怕，从来不敢违抗他的意志。可是今天晚上他要把我嫁给一个年龄大我两倍的男人。先生，请你原谅，给你带来了这样的烦恼①。当然，你不会干那种他想强迫你干的疯狂事。但是，你得让我感谢你说的一番同情话。好些日子都没有谁跟我说过这样的话了。"

这时，诗人眼里有的不仅仅是同情。他肯定是个诗人，因为他把伊旺全忘了。这位新遇到的可爱佳人又年轻又貌美，把他给迷住了。她身上的清香令他不由得心潮起伏。他眼里露出一股柔情，直流向她，她也如饥似渴地领受着。

戴维说："我本要花多年时间才能指望有的收获现在十分钟里便可以得到。小姐，我不愿说我同情你；这样说不算实话——我是爱你。现在我还不能请求你爱我，但是且让我把你从这个恶人手里救出来，到一定的时候会产生爱情的。我想我前程远大，不会一辈子当个牧羊人。现在我会全心全意疼爱你，减少你生活的痛苦。小姐，你愿意把命运托付给我吗？"

"哼，你的自我牺牲是出于同情！"

"出于爱。小姐，时间快到了。"

"你会后悔的，你会瞧不起我。"

"我活着的唯一目的是使你幸福，使自己不辜负了你。"

她从斗篷下伸出只柔软的小手，让他握着。

① vexation /vek'seɪʃən/ n.
烦恼，苦恼

may not be so far off as you think. Tell him. Once away from the power of his eyes I may forget."

David went and stood before the marquis. The black figure stirred, and the mocking eyes glanced at the great hall clock.

"Two minutes to spare. A shepherd requires eight minutes to decide whether he will accept a bride of beauty and income! Speak up, shepherd, do you consent to become mademoiselle's husband? "

"Mademoiselle," said David, standing proudly, "has done me the honor to yield to my request that she become my wife."

"Well said! " said the marquis. "You have yet the making of a **courtier**[1] in you, master shepherd. Mademoiselle could have drawn a worse prize, after all. And now to be done with the affair as quick as the Church and the devil will allow! "

He struck the table soundly with his sword hilt. The landlord came, knee-shaking, bringing more candles in the hope of anticipating the great lord's **whims**[2]. "Fetch a priest," said the marquis, "a priest; do you understand? In ten minutes have a priest here, or — "

The landlord dropped his candles and flew.

The priest came, heavy-eyed and **ruffled**[3]. He made David Mignot and Lucie de Verennes man and wife, pocketed a gold piece that the marquis tossed him, and **shuffled**[4] out again into the night.

"Wine," ordered the marquis, spreading his **ominous**[5] fingers at the host.

"Fill glasses," he said, when it was brought. He stood up at the head of the table in the candlelight, a black mountain of **venom**[6] and **conceit**[7], with something like the memory of an old love turned to poison in his eyes, as it fell upon his niece.

"我愿意把终生托付给你,"她说,"而且,爱情也许不像你想的那样遥远。去告诉他吧。只要见不到他眼里的凶光,我也许会忘得一干二净。"

戴维站到侯爵跟前。那黑色的身影动了动,一双冷眼瞧着房间里的大钟。

"提早了两分钟。一位羊倌花八分钟决定了娶不娶一位有财有貌的小姐做新娘。羊倌,你说个明白,愿不愿意做这位小姐的丈夫?"

"小姐瞧得起我,已经答应了做我妻子的请求。"戴维说,仍站着,显得神气十足。

"说得好!"侯爵道,"羊倌,你倒有一套巴结人的本领。本来小姐也许连这个福分也没有。事情现在就办,只要教堂和魔鬼成全你就行!"

① courtier /ˈkɔːtjə/ n. 奉承者,谄媚者

他用剑鞘把桌子敲得咚咚响。店主人忙赶来,两腿直发颤,手里拿着蜡烛,以为老爷还想要,但又不知猜没猜对心意。"去请一位神父来。"侯爵吩咐道,"一位神父,听明白了吗?十分钟内把神父请来,否则……"

② whim /hwɪm/ n. 念头,心意

店主放下蜡烛就跑了。

神父来了,眼睛不大开,还带了些火气。他把戴维·米尼奥与露西·瓦伦结为夫妇,又把侯爵丢给他的一块金币塞进口袋,然后拖着脚步出了店门,消失在夜幕下。

③ ruffled /rʌfld/ a. 生气,恼怒的

④ shuffle /ʃʌfl/ v. 拖着脚走

⑤ ominous /ˈɒmɪnəs/ a. 不祥的,不吉的

"酒!"侯爵边下令边向店主摊开五指,做出那个让人心悸的手势。

"斟满杯!"酒拿来后他说。他站到长桌的上首,烛光下看起来有如一座黑乎乎的山,既可怕,又巍峨。他的目光转向侄女时,带着异样的怨毒,仿佛是旧爱的记忆化作的仇恨。

⑥ venom /ˈvenəm/ n. 恶毒,恶意

⑦ conceit /kənˈsiːt/ n. 自负,自高自大,骄傲自满

"Monsieur Mignot," he said, raising his wineglass, "drink after I say this to you: You have taken to be your wife one who will make your life a foul and **wretched**① thing. The blood in her is an **inheritance**② running black lies and red ruin. She will bring you shame and anxiety. The devil that descended to her is there in her eyes and skin and mouth that stoop even to **beguile**③ a peasant. There is your promise, monsieur poet, for a happy life. Drink your wine. At last, mademoiselle, I am rid of you."

The marquis drank. A little **grievous**④ cry, as if from a sudden wound, came from the girl's lips. David, with his glass in his hand, stepped forward three paces and faced the marquis. There was little of a shepherd in his **bearing**⑤.

"Just now," he said, calmly, "you did me the honor to call me 'monsieur.' May I hope, therefore that my marriage to mademoiselle has placed me somewhat nearer to you in — let us say, reflected rank — has given me the right to stand more as an equal to monseigneur in a certain little piece of business I have in my mind? "

"You may hope, shepherd," sneered the marquis.

"Then," said David, dashing his glass of wine into the **contemptuous**⑥ eyes that mocked him,"perhaps you will **condescend**⑦ to fight me."

The fury of the great lord outbroke in one sudden curse like a blast from a horn. He tore his sword from its black sheath; he called to the **hovering**⑧ landlord: "A sword there, for this **lout**⑨! " He turned to the lady, with a laugh that chilled her heart, and said: "You put much labor upon me, madame. It seems I must find you a husband and make you a widow in the same night."

"I know not sword-play," said David. He flushed to make the

"米尼奥先生，"他举起酒杯说，"你先听我说句话，然后把酒喝下。你今天娶的老婆会使你的日子痛苦而可悲。她是个猪生狗养的坏种，会使你丢脸，使你伤心。恶魔早缠了她的身，她的眼睛、皮肤、嘴巴都透着邪气，会自甘下贱勾引人，哪怕是个庄稼汉。诗人阁下，这就是你向往的幸福生活。喝酒吧。小姐，我总算是甩脱了你。"

侯爵喝了酒。姑娘嘴里发出一声呻吟，似乎是突然受了伤。戴维手拿酒杯，走了三步，正视着侯爵。看他的举止，他并不像牧羊人。

他从容不迫地说："非常荣幸，刚才你称我为'阁下'。由于我与小姐成婚，我的'现有地位'——请允许我使用这个词——与你多少接近了，所以请问我能否指望，和先生平起平坐地了结我心中想的一桩小事呢？"

"你能指望，羊倌。"侯爵讥讽道。

"那么你也许会屈尊与我打一场！"戴维说着把一杯酒直朝鄙夷地看着他的一双眼泼了过去。

侯爵大人顿时火冒三丈，怒骂一声，响得像突然吹响的一声号角。他从黑剑鞘里拔出剑，对傻站着的店主喊道："拿柄剑来，给这乡巴佬！"他又转身对姑娘发出一声令她胆战心惊的狞笑，说："夫人，你给我添了个大麻烦。看来，同一个夜晚我既得给你找一个丈夫，又得使你变成寡妇。"

"我不会击剑，"戴维说。在自己的妻子面前

① wretched /'retʃɪd/ a. 不幸的，可怜的

② inheritance /ɪn'herɪtəns/ n. 遗传

③ beguile /bɪ'gaɪl/ v. 欺骗，诓骗

④ grievous /'griːvəs/ a. 难忍受的，极痛苦的

⑤ bearing /'beərɪŋ/ n. 举止，风度

⑥ contemptuous /kən'temptjuəs/ a. 瞧不起的，藐视的

⑦ condescend /ˌkɒndɪ'send/ v. 不摆架子，屈尊

⑧ hover /'hɒvə/ v. 徘徊在近旁

⑨ lout /laʊt/ n. 笨拙的人，乡巴佬

confession before his lady.

"'I know not sword-play,'" **mimicked**[1] the marquis. "Shall we fight like peasants with oaken **cudgels**[2]? *Hola*! Francois, my **pistols**[3]! "

A postilion brought two shining great pistols ornamented with **carven**[4] silver, from the carriage holsters. The marquis tossed one upon the table near David's hand. "To the other end of the table," he cried; "even a shepherd may pull a trigger. Few of them attain the honor to die by the weapon of a De Beaupertuys."

The shepherd and the marquis faced each other from the ends of the long table. The landlord, in an ague of terror, **clutched**[5] the air and **stammered**[6]: "M-M-Monseigneur, for the love of Christ! not in my house! — do not spill blood — it will ruin my custom — " The look of the marquis, threatening him, paralyzed his tongue.

"Coward," cried the lord of Beaupertuys, "cease chattering your teeth long enough to give the word for us, if you can."

Mine host's knees smote the floor. He was without a vocabulary. Even sounds were beyond him. Still, by gestures he seemed to beseech peace in the name of his house and custom.

"I will give the word," said the lady, in a clear voice. She went up to David and kissed him sweetly. Her eyes were sparkling bright, and color had come to her cheek. She stood against the wall, and the two men **levelled**[7] their pistols for her count.

"*Un — deux — trois*! "

The two reports came so nearly together that the candles flickered but once. The marquis stood, smiling, the fingers of his left hand resting, outspread, upon the end of the table. David remained erect, and turned his head very slowly, searching for his wife with his eyes. Then, as a garment falls from where it is hung, he sank, **crumpled**[8], upon the

① mimick /'mɪmɪk/ v. 模仿
② cudgel /'kʌdʒəl/ n. 棍棒
③ pistol /'pɪstl/ n. 手枪
④ carven /'kɑːvn/ a. 雕刻的

⑤ clutch /klʌtʃ/ v. 抓住，攫取
⑥ stammer /'stæmə/ v. 口吃，结巴

⑦ level /'levl/ v. 举（枪等）瞄准

⑧ crumple /'krʌmpl/ v. 倒坍，一蹶不振

说出这话他脸红了。

"'我不会击剑'，"侯爵学着他的腔调说，"那么我们难道要学庄稼汉的样，用橡木棍打？来呀！弗朗索瓦，我的手枪！"

一名侍从到马车里拿来两支闪亮、镶银的大手枪。侯爵把一支扔到戴维手边的桌上。"站到桌子那头去！"他叫道，"放羊的也该会扣扳机。能有幸死在博贝尔杜依家人枪口下的放羊人还没几个哩。"

牧羊人与侯爵面对面，各站在长桌的一端。店主吓得浑身筛糠，结结巴巴地说："侯——侯——侯爵，看在上帝面子上！别在我店里！流不得血啊！我的生意就完……"侯爵朝他狠狠一瞪眼，他便哑了。

"胆小鬼！别再啰啰唆唆，你说得出话就给我们发口令。"

店主扑通跪倒在地上，不但不知说什么好，而且连嗓门也发不出声来，但看他比比画画的手势可以知道，他是在央求别动武，他还要开店，还得有客人上门。

"我来发口令。"姑娘清脆的声音说。她走到戴维身边，亲热地吻他，眼睛闪亮，面颊出现了红晕。她靠墙站着，两个决斗的人举起枪等她数数。

"一——二——三！"

两支枪几乎完全同时响，烛光只跳动了一次。侯爵站着，在微笑，左手手指叉开放在桌上。戴维保持直立姿势，慢慢转过头，用目光寻找妻子。

floor.

With a little cry of terror and despair, the widowed maid ran and stooped above him. She found his wound, and then looked up with her old look of pale **melancholy**①. "Through his heart," she whispered. "Oh, his heart! "

"Come," boomed the great voice of the marquis, "out with you to the carriage! Daybreak shall not find you on my hands. Wed you shall be again, and to a living husband, this night. The next we come upon, my lady, highwayman or peasant. If the road yields no other, then the **churl**② that opens my gates. Out with you into the carriage! "

The marquis, **implacable**③ and huge, the lady wrapped again in the mystery of her cloak, the postilion bearing the weapons — all moved out to the waiting carriage. The sound of its ponderous wheels rolling away echoed through the **slumbering**④ village. In the hall of the Silver Flagon the distracted landlord wrung his hands above the slain poet's body, while the flames of the four and twenty candles danced and **flickered**⑤ on the table.

THE RIGHT BRANCH

Three leagues, then, the road ran, and turned into a puzzle. It joined with another and a larger road at right angles. David stood, uncertain, for a while, and then took the road to the right.

Whither it led he knew not, but he was resolved to leave Vernoy far behind that night. He travelled a league and then passed a large chateau which showed **testimony**⑥ of recent entertainment. Lights shone from every window; from the great stone gateway ran a tracery of wheel tracks drawn in the dust by the vehicles of the guests.

接着，他像件没挂稳的衣服，掉在地板上，瘫成一堆。

成了寡妇的小姐又害怕又绝望，无力地叫了一声，跑过去蹲下来看他。她找到了他的伤口，然后抬起头，又现出了凄惨的神情。"射穿了他的心脏，"她低声道，"唉，他的心脏！"

"来吧，出来上马车！"侯爵的大嗓门吼着，"不等天亮我非把你脱手不可。今天夜晚一定给你嫁个活生生的丈夫。小姐，下一个我们遇上谁就是谁，强盗也罢，庄稼汉也罢。如果这条路上碰不到人，就嫁给我家开门的那土包子。出来上车吧！"

身材魁伟的侯爵已矢志不移；小姐又披上斗篷，让人莫测高深；侍从拿着武器；几个都走出店门上了等候在外的马车。沉重的车轮声响遍沉睡的小镇，渐渐远去。银瓶旅社的餐厅里，不知所措的店主望着诗人的尸体直搓手，桌上二十四支蜡烛的火焰跳动着，闪烁着。

往右的路

走出九英里地，遇到了一个难题，到了一个岔路口。一条更宽的路与这条成直角相交。戴维站住犹豫了一会儿，然后走上了右边的路。

这条路通到哪儿他不知道，但是他决定在这个夜晚要把弗洛伊远远抛到身后。走了三英里，他经过一座大城堡，这里看来刚刚开过宴会。每一扇窗口都亮着灯，出了大石头城堡门，地上有一道道车轮印，是客人的车留下的。

① melancholy /'melənkəlɪ/ *n.* 忧郁，沮丧

② churl /tʃɜːl/ *n.* 粗野的人
③ implacable /ɪm'plækəbl/ *a.* 不能安抚的，拒绝和解的

④ slumber /'slʌmbə/ *v.* 睡眠，入睡

⑤ flicker /'flɪkə/ *v.* 闪烁，摇曳，忽隐忽现

⑥ testimony /'testɪmənɪ/ *n.* 证据

Three leagues farther and David was weary. He rested and slept for a while on a bed of pine boughs at the roadside. Then up and on again along the unknown way.

Thus for five days he travelled the great road, sleeping upon Nature's **balsamic**① beds or in peasants' ricks, eating of their black, hospitable bread, drinking from streams or the willing cup of the goatherd.

At length he crossed a great bridge and set his foot within the smiling city that has crushed or crowned more poets than all the rest of the world. His breath came quickly as Paris sang to him in a little **undertone**② her vital chant of greeting — the hum of voice and foot and wheel.

High up under the eaves of an old house in the Rue Conti, David paid for lodging, and set himself, in a wooden chair, to his poems. The street, once sheltering citizens of import and consequence, was now given over to those who ever follow in the wake of decline.

The houses were tall and still possessed of a ruined **dignity**③, but many of them were empty save for dust and the spider. By night there was the clash of steel and the cries of brawlers straying restlessly from inn to inn. Where once gentility abode was now but a rancid and rude incontinence. But here David found housing **commensurate**④ to his scant purse. Daylight and candlelight found him at pen and paper.

One afternoon he was returning from a **foraging**⑤ trip to the lower world, with bread and **curds**⑥ and a bottle of thin wine. Halfway up his dark stairway he met — or rather came upon, for she rested on the stair — a young woman of a beauty that should **balk**⑦ even the justice of a poet's imagination. A loose, dark cloak, flung open, showed a rich gown beneath. Her eyes changed swiftly with every little shade of

再走九英里，戴维觉得很累了。他倒在路边一堆松树枝上睡了一会儿。醒过来后又沿着这条陌生的路往前赶。

就这样，渴了喝口小河的水或者向放羊人讨杯水，饿了吃好客的庄稼人招待的黑面包，夜晚地当床，或者睡农家的干草堆，他沿着这条大路接连走了五天。

① balsamic /bɔːlˈsæmɪk/ a. 香脂的，含香脂的

终于他过了一座大桥，踏进了向往的城市。全世界这儿造就的诗人最多，毁灭的诗人也最多。巴黎用低沉的音调向他反复哼着欢迎曲——由人声、脚步声、车轮声组成的欢迎曲，听得他不由呼吸急促起来。

② undertone /ˈʌndətəʊn/ n. 低声，小声

戴维在康蒂路一所老房子靠顶的阁楼里租了间房，坐到一张木头椅上开始写诗。这条路上原来住的人高贵显赫，现在住的人已没落颓靡。

③ dignity /ˈdɪgnɪtɪ/ n. 尊严，庄严

屋子很高，气派不减当年，但已经破败，许多房间除了落的灰尘和挂的蜘蛛网，已空空如也。入夜以后听到的是铁器叮当的撞击声，不安分的醉汉出入酒店的叫骂声。昔日贵胄名门的住地今天已沦为藏污纳垢之所。但戴维囊中羞涩，而这里正好房租低廉。他不分日夜，笔耕不辍。

④ commensurate /kəˈmenʃərət/ a. 相当的，相称的
⑤ foraging /ˈfɒrɪdʒɪŋ/ a. 觅食的
⑥ curd /kɜːd/ n. 凝乳
⑦ balk /bɔːk/ v. 阻止，阻碍，妨碍

一天下午，他下楼买了东西回来，拿着面包、酸奶和一瓶劣酒。黑乎乎的楼梯上了一半时，他遇上了——或者不如说撞着了，因为那人坐在楼梯上没动——一个年轻姑娘，一个美得让诗人的想象都苍白无力的姑娘。她披的那件黑色斗篷很大，敞开着，露出了里面华贵的长衫。她的眼神随着思绪的每一细小变化而迅速变化。片

thought. Within one moment they would be rou nd and artless like a child's, and long and **cozening**① like a gypsy's. One hand raised her gown, undraping a little shoe, high-heeled, with its **ribbons**② dangling, untied. So heavenly she was, so unfitted to stoop, so qualified to charm and command! Perhaps she had seen David coming, and had waited for his help there.

Ah, would monsieur pardon that she occupied the stairway, but the shoe! — the naughty shoe! Alas! it would not remain tied. Ah! if monsieur *would* be so gracious!

The poet's fingers trembled as he tied the contrary ribbons. Then he would have fled from the danger of her presence, but the eyes grew long and cozening, like a gypsy's, and held him. He leaned against the balustrade, clutching his bottle of sour wine.

"You have been so good," she said, smiling. "Does monsieur, perhaps, live in the house?"

"Yes, madame. I — I think so, madame."

"Perhaps in the third story, then?"

"No, madame; higher up."

The lady fluttered her fingers with the least possible gesture of impatience.

"Pardon. Certainly I am not discreet in asking. Monsieur will forgive me? It is surely not becoming that I should inquire where he lodges."

"Madame, do not say so. I live in the —"

"No, no, no; do not tell me. Now I see that I erred. But I cannot lose the interest I feel in this house and all that is in it. Once it was my home. Often I come here but to dream of those happy days again. Will you let that be my excuse? "

① cozen /'kʌzn/ v. 骗取，哄
骗
② ribbon /'rɪbən/ n. 缎带，丝
带

刻之间，一双睁得圆圆的、像孩子般天真无邪的
眼会眯缝起来，变得像吉普赛人那般诡诈。她的
一只手撩开了长衫，露出只高跟小鞋，鞋带没系
上，耷拉着。她有如天仙，不能屈尊，只会迷倒
你，主宰你。也许她早看见了戴维上来，在等着
他去帮一把。

唉，高贵的先生一定会原谅她挡在楼梯上，
其实只为了一只鞋！捣蛋的鞋！咳，鞋带总不能
不系上！哟，只要先生心好！

诗人在系鞋带时手指颤抖着。系好以后他本
想逃之夭夭，但是那双眼眯起来，像吉普赛人的
一样充满诡诈，叫他拔不了腿。他靠在扶手上，
紧紧抓着瓶酒。

"你真是个大好人，"她笑着说，"大概先生
是住在这房子里的吧?"

"对，小姐。我——我想是，小姐。"

"那么也许住三楼?"

"不，小姐。还要往上。"

姑娘的手指摆了摆，但这不可能是急躁的表
示。

"对不起。我真是太冒昧，不该问。先生能包
涵吗? 我打听别人的住处，这实在有失体统。"

"小姐，别这样说。我住在……"

"不，不，不，你别告诉我。现在我知道我错
了。可是我还是对这房子感兴趣，对这里的一切
感兴趣。原来我住在这地方。我常来这里，就为
回想往日的快乐。你能接受我这个理由吗?"

"Let me tell you, then, for you need no excuse," stammered the poet. "I live in the top floor — the small room where the stairs turn."

"In the front room? " asked the lady, turning her head sidewise.

"The rear, madame."

The lady **sighed**[1], as if with relief.

"I will detain you no longer then, monsieur," she said, employing the round and artless eye. "Take good care of my house. Alas! only the memories of it are mine now. Adieu, and accept my thanks for your **courtesy**[2]."

She was gone, leaving but a smile and a trace of sweet perfume. David climbed the stairs as one in slumber. But he awoke from it, and the smile and the perfume lingered with him and never afterward did either seem quite to leave him. This lady of whom he knew nothing drove him to lyrics of eyes, **chansons**[3] of swiftly conceived love, odes to curling hair, and sonnets to slippers on slender feet.

Poet he must have been, for Yvonne was forgotten; this fine, new loveliness held him with its freshness and grace. The subtle perfume about her filled him with strange emotions.

* * * * *

On a certain night three persons were gathered about a table in a room on the third floor of the same house. Three chairs and the table and a lighted candle upon it was all the furniture. One of the persons was a huge man, dressed in black. His expression was one of sneering pride. The ends of his upturned moustache reached nearly to his mocking eyes. Another was a lady, young and beautiful, with eyes that could be round and artless, as a child's, or long and cozening, like a gypsy's, but were

"让我来告诉你吧，你用不着说什么理由。"诗人有些结结巴巴了，"我住在顶层，是……是那间楼梯转弯处的小房间。"

"是前房？"小姐问，把头侧向了一边。

"后房，小姐。"

小姐轻舒口气，像是放下了一桩心事。

"先生，那我就不耽误你了。"她说，眼睛圆而天真无邪，"要爱惜我的房子啊。唉，现在属于我的只有记忆了。再见，感谢先生你帮忙。"

她走了，仅仅留下一个微笑和一阵芳香。戴维痴痴呆呆往楼上爬。但他又清醒过来，那微笑、那芳香还伴随着他，后来似乎也一直跟着他。这位他毫不了解的姑娘使他诗兴大发，想到了佳句描绘眼睛，歌颂一见倾心的爱，赞美鬈发，吟咏穿在秀气的脚上的拖鞋。

他肯定是个诗人，因为他把伊旺全忘了。这位新遇到的可爱佳人又年轻又貌美，把他给迷住了。她身上的芳香令他不由得心潮起伏。

* * *

某天夜晚，也是这所房子。三楼一间房的桌边围坐着三个人。房内的摆设就是三把椅子，那张桌子，还有桌上燃着的蜡烛。三人中有一个身躯魁伟，穿黑衣裳。他满脸瞧不起人的高傲神气。八字胡高高翘起，两端几乎碰着了傲气十足的眼睛。还有一位姑娘，年轻美貌，一双眼既能睁得圆圆的，像孩子般天真无邪，又能眯缝起来，像

① sigh /saɪ/ v. 叹气，叹息

② courtesy /'kɜːtɪsɪ/ n. 礼貌，殷勤

③ chanson /'ʃænsən/ n. （法语）歌，小歌曲

now keen and ambitious, like any other **conspirator**[①]'s. The third was a man of action, a **combatant**[②], a bold and impatient **executive**[③], breathing fire and steel. He was addressed by the others as Captain Desrolles.

This man struck the table with his fist, and said, with controlled violence:

"To-night. To-night as he goes to midnight mass. I am tired of the plotting that gets nowhere. I am sick of signals and **ciphers**[④] and secret meetings and such *baragouin*. Let us be honest **traitors**[⑤]. If France is to be rid of him, let us kill in the open, and not hunt with **snares**[⑥] and traps. To-night, I say. I back my words. My hand will do the deed. To-night, as he goes to mass."

The lady turned upon him a cordial look. Woman, however wedded to plots, must ever thus bow to rash courage. The big man stroked his upturned moustache.

"Dear captain," he said, in a great voice, softened by habit, "this time I agree with you. Nothing is to be gained by waiting. Enough of the palace guards belong to us to make the **endeavor**[⑦] a safe one."

"To-night," repeated Captain Desrolles, again striking the table. "You have heard me, marquis; my hand will do the deed."

"But now," said the huge man, softly, "comes a question. Word must be sent to our **partisans**[⑧] in the palace, and a signal agreed upon. Our **stanchest**[⑨] men must accompany the royal carriage. At this hour what messenger can **penetrate**[⑩] so far as the south doorway? Ribouet is stationed there; once a message is placed in his hands, all will go well."

"I will send the message," said the lady.

① conspirator /kən'spɪrətə/ *n.* 阴谋者，共谋者

② combatant /'kɒmbətənt/ *n.* 参加战斗者

③ executive /ɪg'zekjʊtɪv/ *n.* 执行者；行政官；高级官员

④ cipher /'saɪfə/ *n.* 密码；密码文件

⑤ traitor /'treɪtə/ *n.* 叛徒，卖国贼

⑥ snare /sneə/ *n.* (捕捉鸟兽等的)陷阱，罗网

⑦ endeavor /ɪn'devə/ *n.* 努力，尽力

⑧ partisan /ˌpɑːtɪ'zæn/ *n.* (党派等的)铁杆支持者

⑨ stanch /stɑːntʃ/ *a.* 可靠的，坚定的

⑩ penetrate /'penɪtreɪt/ *v.* 穿过，刺入，透过

吉普赛人那般诡诈，不过现在它们像所有玩阴谋的人的眼一样，闪着蠢蠢欲动的光。第三位是动手干的人，一位斗士，一位大胆、急躁的汉子，脾气火爆，性子刚猛。另外两个称他为德斯罗尔上尉。

这人用拳头擂着桌子，强压住火气说：

"就在今晚，今晚趁他午夜去做弥撒时。我才不耐烦那些不顶用的计谋。我讨厌什么打信号、用密语、开密会这些名堂。我们要背叛就堂堂正正背叛。如果法兰西要除掉他，那我们就公开杀，何必暗地里设圈套、陷阱。我看该在今晚。我的话不是儿戏。我要亲手结果了他。就在今晚，趁他去做弥撒时。"

姑娘向他投过去一道赞许的目光。女人无论怎样工于心计，也会像她一样佩服鲁莽人的勇气。大个子摸摸他的翘八字胡。

"上尉先生，"他说，音量大而声气惯来柔和，"这一次我同意你的看法。等待得不到任何结果。宫廷侍卫中有足够的人站在我们这一边，干起来没问题。"

"就在今晚。"德斯罗尔上尉重复说，又擂桌子，"侯爵，我说话算话。我要亲手结果了他。"

"可是现在还有一个问题。"大个子声气柔和地说，"要给宫廷里我们一边的人送信，暗号要统一。陪伴銮舆的一定要是我们最可靠的人。到了现在这时候能派谁直抵南门送信呢？南门值勤的是里博，只要把信送到他手里，一切都好办。"

"我去送信。"那姑娘说。

"You, countess?" said the marquis, raising his eyebrows. "Your devotion is great, we know, but —"

"Listen!" **exclaimed**[①] the lady, rising and resting her hands upon the table; "in a garret of this house lives a youth from the provinces as guileless and tender as the lambs he tended there. I have met him twice or thrice upon the stairs. I questioned him, fearing that he might dwell too near the room in which we are accustomed to meet. He is mine, if I will. He writes poems in his garret, and I think he dreams of me. He will do what I say. He shall take the message to the palace."

The marquis rose from his chair and bowed. "You did not permit me to finish my sentence, countess," he said. "I would have said: 'Your devotion is great, but your wit and charm are **infinitely**[②] greater.'"

While the conspirators were thus engaged, David was polishing some lines addressed to his *amorette d'escalier*. He heard a timorous knock at his door, and opened it, with a great throb, to behold her there, panting as one in straits, with eyes wide open and artless, like a child's.

"Monsieur," she breathed, "I come to you in distress. I believe you to be good and true, and I know of no other help. How I flew through the streets among the **swaggering**[③] men! Monsieur, my mother is dying. My uncle is a captain of guards in the palace of the king. Some one must fly to bring him. May I hope —"

"Mademoiselle," interrupted Davis, his eyes shining with the desire to do her service, "your hopes shall be my wings. Tell me how I may reach him."

The lady thrust a **sealed**[④] paper into his hand.

"Go to the south gate — the south gate, mind — and say to the guards there, 'The **falcon**[⑤] has left his nest.' They will pass you, and

① exclaim /ɪksˈkleɪm/ v. (由于兴奋,痛苦等)呼喊,惊叫

② infinitely /ˈɪnfɪnɪtlɪ/ ad. 无限地,无穷地;极其地

③ swagger /ˈswæɡə/ v. 昂首阔步,大摇大摆地走

④ seal /siːl/ v. 封上(信封)

⑤ falcon /ˈfɔːlkən/ n. 隼,猎鹰

"要劳你伯爵夫人大驾?"侯爵竖起眉毛说,"你忠心耿耿,这我们知道,但是……"

"你听我说!"伯爵夫人说着站起身,双手放在桌上,"这房子的一间小阁楼里住着个外省来的年轻人,天真温顺得跟他在外省放的羊一样。我在楼梯上遇见过他两三次。我怕他住得靠我们每次碰头的房间太近,特意套过他的话。只要我愿意,他就是我的人。他在阁楼里写诗,看来他对我是夜思梦想。我说的话他会照办。到王宫送信派他去。"

侯爵从椅上站起来一鞠躬,说:"夫人,你没让我把话说完。我本想说你忠心耿耿,但更千金难买的是你的智慧和美貌。"

当这几个阴谋家定下大计时,戴维正在为他写的诗《楼梯上的爱神》润色。他听到有人轻轻敲了一下门。打开一看,心猛地一跳,因为他发现敲门的原来是她,气吁吁的,像有为难事,两眼大睁着,跟孩子一样天真无邪。

她说:"先生,我是来求你帮忙的。我知道你是个诚实的好人,除了你没人能帮我。我是一路上挤过人群飞跑来的。先生,我母亲已经病危。我叔叔在王宫当侍卫长。非得请个人赶快给他捎信不可。我希望……"

"小姐,你的希望就是我的翅膀。告诉我怎么到他那儿。"戴维打断她的话,眼睛发亮,巴不得为她效劳。

姑娘把一封已封好的信塞到他手里。

you will go to the south entrance to the palace. Repeat the words, and give this letter to the man who will reply 'Let him strike when he will.' This is the password, monsieur, entrusted to me by my uncle, for now when the country is disturbed and men plot against the king's life, no one without it can gain entrance to the palace grounds after nightfall. If you will, monsieur, take him this letter so that my mother may see him before she closes her eyes."

"Give it me," said David, eagerly. "But shall I let you return home through the streets alone so late? I — "

"No, no — fly. Each moment is like a precious jewel. Some time," said the lady, with eyes long and cozening, like a gypsy's, "I will try to thank you for your goodness."

The poet thrust the letter into his breast, and bounded down the stairway. The lady, when he was gone, returned to the room below.

The eloquent eyebrows of the marquis **interrogated**① her.

"He is gone," she said, "as fleet and stupid as one of his own sheep, to deliver it."

The table shook again from the batter of Captain Desrolles's fist.

"Sacred name! " he cried; "I have left my pistols behind! I can trust no others."

"Take this," said the marquis, drawing from beneath his cloak a shining, great weapon, ornamented with carven silver. "There are none truer. But guard it closely, for it bears my arms and crest, and already I am suspected. Me, I must put many leagues between myself and Paris this night. To-morrow must find me in my chateau. After you, dear countess."

The marquis puffed out the candle. The lady, well cloaked, and the two gentlemen softly descended the stairway and flowed into the crowd

"你去王宫的南门。记着，是南门。对卫兵说'鹰离了巢'，他们会放你过去。然后从南面入口进王宫。然后再说那句话，听到有人回答'它想出击就让它出击'你便把这封信交给他。先生，这是我叔叔教给我的暗语，因为现在国家动荡，有人阴谋刺杀国王，午夜以后不说出暗语谁也别想进宫。先生，有劳你把这封信带给他，让我母亲见他一面，死能瞑目。"

"交给我好了。"戴维急切地说，"不过天这么晚，你一个人回家走在街上能行吗？我……"

"用不着，用不着。你快走。片刻时间就像一颗珍宝一样贵重。以后我会想办法回报你的好心。"姑娘的眼眯了起来，像吉普赛人的那样诡诈。

诗人把信往胸口一塞，快步下楼。等他走后，姑娘回到下面房间。

① interrogate /ɪnˈterəɡeɪt/ v.
审问，质问

侯爵扬起会说话的眉毛，看着她。

"他去送信了，跟他自己放的羊一样，腿快脑子笨。"

德斯罗尔上尉又一拳打得桌子晃荡。

"糟糕！"他嚷道，"我没带手枪！别的枪我信不过。"

"拿这把去。"侯爵说着从斗篷里掏出一把大家伙，镶着银，"这把最牢靠。不过你拿着千万要小心，枪上有我的纹章与徽号，我又是早就被怀疑上了的人。今晚我得远远地离开巴黎，明天要待在自己城堡。请先，伯爵夫人。"

侯爵吹灭蜡烛。那女的裹好斗篷，与两个男

that roamed along the narrow pavements of the Rue Conti.

David sped. At the south gate of the king's residence a **halberd**[1] was laid to his breast, but he turned its point with the words; "The falcon has left his nest."

"Pass, brother," said the guard, "and go quickly."

On the south steps of the palace they moved to seize him, but again the *mot de passe* charmed the watchers. One among them stepped forward and began: "Let him strike — " but a flurry among the guards told of a surprise. A man of **keen**[2] look and soldierly stride suddenly pressed through them and seized the letter which David held in his hand. "Come with me," he said, and led him inside the great hall. Then he tore open the letter and read it. He beckoned to a man uniformed as an officer of musketeers, who was passing. "Captain Tetreau, you will have the guards at the south entrance and the south gate arrested and confined. Place men known to be loyal in their places." To David he said: "Come with me."

He conducted him through a corridor and an anteroom into a spacious chamber, where a melancholy man, **somberly**[3] dressed, sat brooding in a great, leather-covered chair. To that man he said:

"Sire, I have told you that the palace is as full of traitors and spies as a **sewer**[4] is of rats. You have thought, sire, that it was my fancy. This man penetrated to your very door by their **connivance**[5]. He bore a letter which I have intercepted. I have brought him here that your **majesty**[6] may no longer think my zeal **excessive**[7]."

"I will question him," said the king, stirring in his chair. He looked at David with heavy eyes **dulled**[8] by an opaque film. The poet bent his knee.

"From where do you come?" asked the king.

① halberd /ˈhælbəd/ *n.* 戟

② keen /kiːn/ *a.* 敏锐的,敏捷的;精明的

③ somberly /ˈsɒmbəlɪ/ *ad.* 昏暗地,阴沉地

④ sewer /ˈsjuə(r)/ *n.* 下水道,阴沟

⑤ connivance /kəˈnaɪvəns/ *n.* 默许,纵容

⑥ majesty /ˈmædʒɪstɪ/ *n.* 陛下

⑦ excessive /ɪkˈsesɪv/ *a.* 过度的,过分的

⑧ dull /dʌl/ *v.* 使迟钝;使阴暗

的轻轻下楼,消失在康蒂路人来人往的狭窄的人行道上。

戴维一路快步。走到王宫南门,一根戟把他当胸拦住,但他对用戟尖顶住他的人说:"鹰离了巢。"

"进去,兄弟。你快走!"卫士说。

在王宫南面的台阶上的卫兵又过来拦他,但他的暗语再次在这些人身上起了作用。有一个上前说:"它想出击……"可是侍卫中起了一阵骚动,看来是出了意外。这时一个模样机警的人突然推开侍卫,威风凛凛大步过来,一把抢过戴维捏在手里的信。"你跟我来。"说着,他把戴维领进了大厅,立即拆开信看了一遍。他看到一位身着步兵军官服的人正走过来,向他招招手,把他叫到跟前,说:"泰特罗上尉,你把南门的侍卫全部逮捕关押,改派忠实可靠的人把守。"又对戴维说:"你跟我来。"

他领戴维经过一道走廊,一间外室,进了一间宽敞的卧室,只见一张大皮革椅上坐了个人,满面愁容,衣服也颜色暗淡,正沉思着。领路的人对那人说:

"陛下,臣曾言宫内逆贼奸细多如牛毛,陛下以为臣言过其实。此人就是乱臣贼子密谋派遣入宫的。现截得密信一封,人也已带来。臣是否言过其实,请陛下明察。"

"让朕亲自审问。"国王在椅上挪了挪身子说。他抬起一双因起了内障而变得无神的眼睛看着戴维。诗人跪了下来。

"你是哪里人?"国王问。

"From the village of Vernoy, in the province of Eure-et-Loir, sire."

"What do you follow in Paris? "

"I — I would be a poet, sire."

"What did you in Vernoy? "

"I minded my father's flock of sheep."

The king stirred again, and the film lifted from his eyes.

"Ah! in the fields! "

"Yes, sire."

"You lived in the fields; you went out in the cool of the morning and lay among the **hedges**① in the grass. The flock **distributed**② itself upon the hillside; you drank of the living stream; you ate your sweet, brown bread in the shade, and you listened, doubtless, to blackbirds **piping**③ in the grove. Is not that so, shepherd? "

"It is, sire," answered David, with a sigh; "and to the bees at the flowers, and, maybe, to the grape gatherers singing on the hill."

"Yes, yes," said the king, impatiently; "maybe to them; but surely to the blackbirds. They whistled often, in the grove, did they not? "

"Nowhere, sire, so sweetly as in Eure-et-Loir. I have endeavored to express their song in some verses that I have written."

"Can you repeat those verses? " asked the king, eagerly. "A long time ago I listened to the blackbirds. It would be something better than a kingdom if one could rightly **construe**④ their song. And at night you drove the sheep to the fold and then sat, in peace and **tranquillity**⑤, to your pleasant bread. Can you repeat those verses, shepherd? "

"They run this way, sire," said David, with respectful ardor:

"'Lazy shepherd, see your **lambkins**⑥

"厄尔卢瓦尔省弗洛伊镇人，陛下。"

"为什么事到了巴黎？"

"我——我想当诗人，陛下。"

"你在弗洛伊干什么呢？"

"我给父亲放羊。"

国王又挪了挪身子，眼睛的内障消失了。

"嗯？是在乡下吗？"

"是，陛下。"

"你以前住在乡下，每天早上天亮出门，自己躺在青草堆里，让羊群满山跑。你喝的是徐徐流水，饿了在树荫下吃香甜的黑面包。你肯定还能听到山鸟在树林里唱歌。是这么回事吗，牧羊人？"

戴维舒了口气，回答道："是，陛下。还听花丛中的蜜蜂唱，有时还听山上摘葡萄的人唱。"

"知道，知道，有时还会听这些人唱，可是少不了要听山鸟唱。"国王不耐烦地说，"那些鸟常会在树林里吹口哨，对吗？"

"陛下，哪儿的鸟也比不上厄尔卢瓦尔的唱得动听。我写过一些诗，想用诗来表达鸟儿的歌唱了什么。"

"这些诗你还记得吗？"国王兴致勃勃地问，"很久以前我听过山鸟唱。按鸟儿的歌写成的诗比江山社稷还要叫人喜爱。晚上你把羊赶进栏，然后坐下吃香喷喷的面包，无忧无虑，无牵无挂，是吗？牧羊人，你还记得那些诗吗？"

"陛下，我还记得。"戴维说着毕恭毕敬且有声有色地朗诵起来。

　　　"懒惰的牧羊人，你看

① hedge /hedʒ/ *n.* 树篱，篱笆

② distribute /dɪˈstrɪbjʊt/ *v.* 分散

③ pipe /paɪp/ *v.* 发尖声，尖声唱

④ construe /kənˈstruː/ *v.* 解释，理解为

⑤ tranquility /træŋˈkwɪlɪtɪ/ *n.* 平静，安静，安宁

⑥ lambkin /ˈlæmkɪn/ *n.* 小羊；宝贝（对孩子等的爱称）

Skip, **ecstatic**①, on the mead;

See the firs dance in the breezes,

Hear Pan blowing at his reed.

Hear us calling from the tree-tops,

See us swoop upon your flock;

Yield us wool to make our nests warm

In the branches of the — '

"If it please your majesty," interrupted a harsh voice, "I will ask a question or two of this rhymester. There is little time to spare. I crave pardon, sire, if my anxiety for your safety offends."

"The loyalty," said the king, "of the Duke d'Aumale is too well proven to give offence." He sank into his chair, and the film came again over his eyes.

"First," said the duke, I will read you the letter he brought:

"'To-night is the anniversary of the dauphin's death. If he goes, as is his custom, to midnight mass to pray for the soul of his son, the falcon will strike, at the corner of the Rue Esplanade. If this be his intention, set a red light in the upper room at the southwest corner of the palace, that the falcon may take heed.'

"Peasant," said the duke, sternly, "you have heard these words. Who gave you this message to bring? "

"My lord duke," said David, sincerely, "I will tell you. A lady gave it me. She said her mother was ill, and that this writing would fetch her uncle to her bedside. I do not know the meaning of the letter, but I will swear that she is beautiful and good."

"Describe the woman," commanded the duke, "and how you came to be her **dupe**②."

"Describe her! " said David with a tender smile. "You would

① ecstatic /ek'stætɪk/ *a.* 狂喜的;着迷的

你的羊群在草上跳得欢;

你看枞树在微风中起舞,

你听牧羊神在吹芦笛。

你听我们在树梢鸣叫,

你看我们掠过你的羊群;

给我们羊毛吧,让我们筑起暖窝,

在树枝的……"

一个刺耳的声音插了进来:"启禀陛下,请让臣问这位吟诗的人一个问题。所剩的时间已经不多。臣为陛下安危深感忧虑,如陛下见责于臣,臣自甘领罪。"

国王说:"多马尔公爵忠心可鉴,何罪之有?"他往椅上一靠,眼睛又起了层内障。

公爵说:"先请陛下让臣念过他带的信。"

"今晚太子死去整整一年。如他照例午夜去做弥撒为儿子的灵魂祈祷,鹰将在游乐场路出击。如他确有此打算,请在王宫西南角楼上悬一红灯,鹰认此为号。"

公爵声色俱厉地说:"庄稼人,这些话你已亲耳听到。是谁叫你捎的信?"

"公爵大人,我可以告诉你。"戴维说,一副老实相,"是位小姐给我的信。她说她母亲生病,送这封信是为了叫叔叔与她母亲见最后一面。我不明白信的意图,但我起誓,她又漂亮又善良。"

"那你描述一下这女人的模样,再说你怎样上了她的当。"公爵命令道。

② dupe /dju:p/ *n.* (不知不觉中)受人操纵的傀儡,被人利用的工具

"描述她的模样!"戴维脸上浮起动情的微笑,"你这是强迫语言创造奇迹。她既有太阳

command words to perform miracles. Well, she is made of sunshine and deep shade. She is slender, like the alders, and moves with their grace. Her eyes change while you gaze into them; now round, and then half shut as the sun peeps between two clouds. When she comes, heaven is all about her; when she leaves, there is chaos and a **scent**② of **hawthorn**① blossoms. She came to see me in the Rue Conti, number twenty-nine."

"It is the house," said the duke, turning to the king, "that we have been watching. Thanks to the poet's tongue, we have a picture of the infamous Countess Quebedaux."

"Sire and my lord duke," said David, **earnestly**③, "I hope my poor words have done no injustice. I have looked into that lady's eyes. I will stake my life that she is an angel, letter or no letter."

The duke looked at him steadily. "I will put you to the proof," he said, slowly. "Dressed as the king, you shall, yourself, attend mass in his carriage at midnight. Do you accept the test? "

David smiled. "I have looked into her eyes," he said. "I had my proof there. Take yours how you will."

Half an hour before twelve the Duke d'Aumale, with his own hands, set a red lamp in a southwest window of the palace. At ten minutes to the hour, David, leaning on his arm, dressed as the king, from top to toe, with his head bowed in his cloak, walked slowly from the royal apartments to the waiting carriage. The duke assisted him inside and closed the door. The carriage **whirled**④ away along its route to the cathedral.

On the *qui vive* in a house at the corner of the Rue Esplanade was Captain Tetreau with twenty men, ready to **pounce**⑤ upon the conspirators when they should appear.

的温暖，又有树荫的阴凉。她静似杨柳立，动如杨柳拂。你仔细观察她的眼睛，会发现它们变化多端，一会儿圆，一会儿半开半闭，好比太阳躲在两朵云间。她来时如天仙下凡，走时使你茫然若失，只留下一阵山楂花香。是她到康蒂路二十九号来找我的。"

公爵转身对国王说："就是我们监视的那屋子。亏得诗人嘴巧，把那臭名昭著的凯贝多伯爵夫人的模样说得清清楚楚。"

"陛下，公爵大人，我希望我拙劣的言辞没有夸大事实。我观察过这位小姐的眼睛。我可以起誓，她美如天仙，这与捎不捎信无关。"戴维说的是肺腑之言。

公爵眼也不眨地看着他，慢慢说道："我要试试你的真假。今天午夜你就穿上国王的衣服，乘坐銮舆去做弥撒。你愿意试吗？"

戴维微微一笑，说："我观察过了她的眼睛。我从她眼里看出了真假。你要怎么试就试吧。"

离午夜差半小时时，多马尔公爵亲手在王宫西南角窗口挂起一盏红灯。十二点差十分时，戴维周身上下换上了国王的穿戴，把头埋进斗篷里，由公爵扶着，缓缓步出王宫，来到等候在外的銮舆前。公爵扶他进舆，关上门。銮舆起步了，一直向教堂驶去。

在游乐场路的转弯处泰特罗上尉带领二十名手下人等在一所房子里，一见阴谋分子露面便立即捉拿。

① scent /sent/ *n.* 气味,香味
② hawthorn /'hɔ:θɔ:n/ *n.* 山楂

③ earnestly /'ɜ:nɪstlɪ/ *ad.* 认真地,诚挚地

④ whirl /hwɜ:l/ *v.* 回旋,急驶

⑤ pounce /paʊns/ *v.* 猛扑,突然袭击

But it seemed that, for some reason, the plotters had slightly altered their plans. When the royal carriage had reached the Rue Christopher, one square nearer than the Rue Esplanade, forth from it burst Captain Desrolles, with his band of would-be **regicides**①, and **assailed**② the **equipage**③. The guards upon the carriage, though surprised at the **premature**④ attack, descended and fought **valiantly**⑤. The noise of conflict attracted the force of Captain Tetreau, and they came **pelting**⑥ down the street to the rescue. But, in the meantime, the desperate Desrolles had torn open the door of the king's carriage, thrust his weapon against the body of the dark figure inside, and fired.

Now, with loyal **reinforcements**⑦ at hand, the street rang with cries and the rasp of steel, but the frightened horses had dashed away. Upon the cushions lay the dead body of the poor mock king and poet, slain by a ball from the pistol of Monseigneur, the Marquis de Beaupertuys.

THE MAIN ROAD

Three leagues, then, the road ran, and turned into a puzzle. It joined with another and a larger road at right angles. David stood, uncertain, for a while, and then sat himself to rest upon its side.

Whither these roads led he knew not. Either way there seemed to lie a great world full of chance and peril. And then, sitting there, his eye fell upon a bright star, one that he and Yvonne had named for theirs. That set him thinking of Yvonne, and he wondered if he had not been too hasty. Why should he leave her and his home because a few hot words had come between them? Was love so **brittle**⑧ a thing that jealousy, the very proof of it, could break it? Mornings always brought

① regicide /'redʒɪsaɪd/ *n.* 弑君者(或行为)

② assail /ə'seɪl/ *v.* 攻击,困扰

③ equipage /'ekwɪpɪdʒ/ *n.* (船舶、军队、探险队等的)装备,用具

④ premature /ˌpriːmə'tjʊə/ *a.* 比预期早的,过早的

⑤ valiantly /'væljəntlɪ/ *ad.* 勇敢地,英勇地

⑥ pelt /pelt/ *v.* (连续地)投掷,开火

⑦ reinforcements /ˌriːɪn'fɔːsmənts/ *n.* 增援部队

⑧ brittle /'brɪtl/ *a.* 易碎的,一碰就破的,易损坏的

然而,不知什么原因,阴谋分子的计划似乎有所变动。当銮舆走到离游乐场路一个十字路口的克里斯托弗路时,德斯罗尔上尉带着帮意图弑君的杀手一拥而上,冲向銮舆。守卫銮舆的侍卫尽管没有料到事情提前发作,还是下车奋战。喊杀的声音惊动泰特罗上尉的一帮人,他们忙飞奔而来增援。然而就在这时,德斯罗尔这亡命之徒已撞开王驾车门,把武器顶着车里黑乎乎的身躯开了火。

接着,忠于王上的增援人员赶到,街上只听到一片喊杀声和刀剑的叮当声。但马受了惊,狂奔而去。銮舆的坐垫上躺着那位假扮国王的倒霉诗人的尸体,他是中了博贝尔杜依侯爵的手枪子弹身亡的。

当中的路

走出九英里地,遇到了一个难题,到了一个岔路口。一条更宽的路与这条成直角相交。戴维站住犹豫了一会儿,然后坐到路边休息。

他不知道两个方向的路通向何处,似乎每个方向都充满机遇又危机四伏。坐下以后他瞧见了一颗明亮的星,他和伊旺曾说这颗星是属于他们的。这一来他思念起伊旺,怀疑自己是否过于莽撞。为什么他要为两人拌了几句嘴而离开她,离开家呢?难道爱情当真脆弱,最能证明它的嫉妒也能叫它完蛋吗?夜晚小小的烦恼到早上总是不医而愈。他回家还来得及,酣睡的弗洛伊镇谁也

a cure for the little heartaches of evening. There was yet time for him to return home without any one in the sweetly sleeping village of Vernoy being the wiser. His heart was Yvonne's; there where he had lived always he could write his poems and find his happiness.

David rose, and shook off his unrest and the wild mood that had **tempted**[1] him. He set his face **steadfastly**[2] back along the road he had come. By the time he had retravelled the road to Vernoy, his desire to rove was gone. He passed the sheepfold, and the sheep **scurried**[3], with a drumming flutter, at his late footsteps, warming his heart by the homely sound. He crept without noise into his little room and lay there, thankful that his feet had escaped the distress of new roads that night.

How well he knew woman's heart! The next evening Yvonne was at the well in the road where the young **congregated**[4] in order that the *cure* might have business. The corner of her eye was engaged in a search for David, albeit her set mouth seemed **unrelenting**[5]. He saw the look; braved the mouth, drew from it a recantation and, later, a kiss as they walked homeward together.

Three months afterwards they were married. David's father was shrewd and prosperous. He gave them a wedding that was heard of three leagues away. Both the young people were favorites in the village. There was a procession in the streets, a dance on the green; they had the **marionettes**[6] and a **tumbler**[7] out from Dreux to delight the guests.

Then a year, and David's father died. The sheep and the cottage descended to him. He already had the **seemliest**[8] wife in the village. Yvonne's milk pails and her brass kettles were bright — *ouf!* they blinded you in the sun when you passed that way. But you must keep your eyes upon her yard, for her flower beds were so neat and gay they

不会知道。他的心是属于伊旺的，在他土生土长的地方他可以写诗，可以找到他的快乐。

戴维站起身，摆脱了烦恼，浇灭了引诱他背井离乡的火气。他毅然决然地转身走上他来的那条路。当他重新回到弗洛伊镇时，远走高飞的打算全没有了。他经过羊栏，羊听到他迟迟归来的脚步声乱窜起来，像在轻轻地乱敲鼓，这家乡熟悉的声音使他感到心里暖烘烘。他悄没声地溜进自己的小房间，躺了下来，暗自庆幸这天晚上逃脱了完全陌生的路上的苦难。

他真了解女人的心！第二天晚上，伊旺到了路旁年轻人聚在一起听神父讲道的井边。她斜着眼在找戴维，虽然嘴紧紧地闭着没动，似乎不想饶人。他看见了她的目光，没害怕她的嘴，在一道回家的路上，从她嘴里得到了一句后悔的话，后来，又得到一个亲吻。

三个月后他们结婚了。戴维的父亲是个精明能干的人，又家业兴旺。他为他们举行了隆重的婚礼，九英里路外都有所风闻。两个年轻人在镇上都人缘好。街上贺喜的人成群，他们在草地上举行了舞会。为了使客人尽兴，他们从德罗请来了木偶剧团和杂技团。

一年后，戴维的父亲去世了，羊群和房子归了戴维。他的妻子在全镇是最贤良的。伊旺的奶桶和铜壶锃亮。你要是出太阳时从桶边、壶边过，你等着瞧，它们会照得你眼发花！但你的眼睛保准离不开她的院子，因为她的花圃又整齐又鲜艳，你不瞧也得瞧。你还可以听到她唱歌，

① tempt /tempt/ v. 引诱，诱惑

② steadfastly /'stedfəstlɪ/ ad. 坚定地

③ scurry /'skɜːrɪ/ v. 急跑，急赶

④ congregate /'kɒŋgrɪˌɡeɪt/ v. 聚集，集合

⑤ unrelenting /ˌʌnrɪ'lentɪŋ/ a. 无情的；不屈不挠的

⑥ marionette /ˌmærɪə'net/ n. 牵线木偶

⑦ tumbler /'tʌmblə/ n. 杂技演员

⑧ seemly /'siːmlɪ/ a. 得体的，合乎礼仪的

restored to you your sight. And you might hear her sing, aye, as far as the double chestnut tree above Pere Gruneau's **blacksmith**① forge.

But a day came when David drew out paper from a long-shut drawer, and began to bite the end of a pencil. Spring had come again and touched his heart. Poet he must have been, for now Yvonne was well-nigh forgotten. This fine new loveliness of earth held him with its witchery and grace. The perfume from her woods and **meadows**② stirred him strangely. Daily had he gone forth with his flock, and brought it safe at night. But now he stretched himself under the hedge and pieced words together on his bits of paper. The sheep strayed, and the wolves, perceiving that difficult poems make easy mutton, **ventured**③ from the woods and stole his lambs.

David's stock of poems grew longer and his flock smaller. Yvonne's nose and temper **waxed**④ sharp and her talk blunt. Her pans and kettles grew dull, but her eyes had caught their flash. She pointed out to the poet that his **neglect**⑤ was reducing the flock and bringing woe upon the household. David hired a boy to guard the sheep, locked himself in the little room at the top of the cottage, and wrote more poems. The boy, being a poet by nature, but not furnished with an outlet in the way of writing, spent his time in slumber. The wolves lost no time in discovering that poetry and sleep are practically the same; so the flock steadily grew smaller. Yvonne's ill temper increased at an equal rate. Sometimes she would stand in the yard and rail at David through his high window. Then you could hear her as far as the double chestnut tree above Pere Gruneau's blacksmith forge.

M. Papineau, the kind, wise, meddling old notary, saw this, as he saw everything at which his nose pointed. He went to David, fortified himself with a great pinch of snuff, and said:

① blacksmith /'blæksmɪθ/ *n.*
铁匠

② meadow /'medəʊ/ *n.* 草地

③ venture /'ventʃə/ *v.* 冒险，
大胆行事

④ wax /wæks/ *v.* 增加，变大

⑤ neglect /nɪg'lekt/ *n.* 忽视，
忽略

歌声一直远远传到佩雷·格鲁诺铁匠铺门前的板栗树。

然而，有一天，戴维终于从久久没打开过的抽屉里拿出了纸，开始咬铅笔杆。春天又来了，激荡着他的心。他肯定是个诗人，这时间他几乎把伊旺忘了。回春的大地真美丽动人，以它的魔力和姿色迷住了戴维。树林里、草地上的清香使他心旷神怡。本来每天他赶着羊出门，晚上平安回家。但现在不同，他躺到小树下，冥思苦想着在纸片上写写涂涂。羊四处乱走。诗难写时羊肉便易吃，狼见有机可乘，大胆窜出树林把小羊偷走了。

戴维的诗越写越多，他的羊却越放越少。伊旺的肝火上升，话变得难听。她的锅子、铜壶失去了光泽，眼倒冒起火星来。她正告诗人，由于他漫不经心，羊越来越少，一个家也跟着遭了殃。戴维雇了个人放羊，干脆闭门不出，守在楼上的一间小房里写诗。戴维雇的人本也有诗人的天性，但不具备写诗的本领，靠睡觉打发时间。狼马上发现贪睡的与爱写诗的没两样。于是，羊日渐减少。伊旺的火气是日渐增加。有时候她会站在院子里，对着楼上的窗口骂戴维，骂声远远传到佩雷·格鲁诺铁匠铺门前的板栗树。

公证人帕皮诺先生是位又好心、又精明、百事都管的老先生，什么都逃不过他的慧眼，他当然把这一切也看在眼里。他登门找到戴维，使劲吸了一口烟，说：

"Friend Mignot, I **affixed**① the seal upon the marriage certificate of your father. It would distress me to be **obliged** ② to attest a paper signifying the **bankruptcy**③ of his son. But that is what you are coming to. I speak as an old friend. Now, listen to what I have to say. You have your heart set, I perceive, upon poetry. At Dreux, I have a friend, one Monsieur Bril — Georges Bril. He lives in a little cleared space in a houseful of books. He is a learned man; he visits Paris each year; he himself has written books. He will tell you when the **catacombs**④ were made, how they found out the names of the stars, and why the plover has a long bill. The meaning and the form of poetry is to him as intelligent as the **baa**⑤ of a sheep is to you. I will give you a letter to him, and you shall take him your poems and let him read them. Then you will know if you shall write more, or give your attention to your wife and business."

"Write the letter," said David, "I am sorry you did not speak of this sooner."

At sunrise the next morning he was on the road to Dreux with the precious roll of poems under his arm. At noon he wiped the dust from his feet at the door of Monsieur Bril. That learned man broke the seal of M. Papineau's letter, and sucked up its contents through his **gleaming** ⑥ spectacles as the sun draws water. He took David inside to his study and sat him down upon a little island beat upon by a sea of books.

Monsieur Bril had a conscience. He **flinched**⑦ not even at a mass of **manuscript**⑧ the thickness of a finger-length and rolled to an **incorrigible**⑨ curve. He broke the back of the roll against his knee and began to read. He slighted nothing; he bored into the lump as a worm into a nut, seeking for a kernel.

Meanwhile, David sat, **marooned**⑩, trembling in the spray of so

① affix /ə'fɪks/ v. 贴上，把
……固定

② oblige /ə'blaɪdʒ/ v. 强使，
迫使

③ bankruptcy /'bæŋkrəptsɪ/
n. 破产，倒闭

④ catacombs /'kætəkəʊmɪ/ n.
地下墓穴

⑤ baa /bɑː/ n. 羊、牛的叫声

⑥ gleaming /gliːmɪŋ/ a. 闪
烁的

⑦ flinch /flɪntʃ/ v. 畏惧，退
缩

⑧ manuscript
/'mænjʊskrɪpt/ n. 手稿；原
稿

⑨ incorrigible /ɪn'kɒrɪdʒəbl/
a. 积习难改的，不可救药
的

⑩ maroon /mə'ruːn/ v. 使处
于孤立无援的境地

　　"米尼奥老弟，你父亲结婚证上的大印还是我盖上的。如果弄得我非得在一张宣告他儿子破产的文书上签字作证不可，那会叫我伤心。但作为你的老朋友我得进一言，你再这样下去就离产不远。我知道，你一心迷上了诗。我在德勒有个朋友，姓布里尔——名字是若尔日·布里尔。他满屋子是书，住的地方倒只有一小块。这人很有学问，每年都要去巴黎，自己也写了书。他能告诉你罗马的墓窖是在什么时间修建的，怎么辨认天上的星星，为什么千鸟嘴长。他对诗歌的意与形内行就像你对羊的叫声内行一样。我写封信把你介绍给他，你把你写的诗带去请他看看，这样你就能知道你该把诗继续写下去呢，还是该把心思放到妻子和家业上来。"

　　戴维说："那您就写吧。可惜的是您没早说起这件事。"

　　第二天早上太阳刚露面，戴维夹着一大卷珍贵的诗稿踏上了去德勒的路。中午时分，他已在布里尔先生的门口掸鞋子上的土了。这位满腹经纶的学者拆开帕皮诺先生信上的封口，戴上擦亮的眼镜仔仔细细地看着信，就像太阳慢慢地晒干水。他把戴维领进书房，让他坐在四周被书海包围的小岛上。

　　布里尔先生善体人心，见到足足有伸长了的指头厚又卷得乱七八糟的手稿也没皱眉。他把稿卷放在膝上摊开读了起来。他什么都没放过，一页页往下看，就像钻进果实里的虫，不爬到果心里不罢休。

　　这时间戴维像是坐着船在广阔的文学海洋里

much literature. It roared in his ears. He held no chart or compass for voyaging in that sea. Half the world, he thought, must be writing books.

Monsieur Bril bored to the last page of the poems. Then he took off his spectacles, and wiped them with his handkerchief.

"My old friend, Papineau, is well? " he asked.

"In the best of health," said David.

"How many sheep have you, Monsieur Mignot? "

"Three hundred and nine, when I counted them yesterday. The flock has had ill fortune. To that number it has decreased from eight hundred and fifty."

"You have a wife and home, and lived in comfort. The sheep brought you plenty. You went into the fields with them and lived in the keen air and ate the sweet bread of **contentment**①. You had but to be **vigilant**② and **recline**③ there upon nature's breast, listening to the whistle of the blackbirds in the grove. Am I right thus far? "

"It was so," said David.

"I have read all your **verses**④," continued Monsieur Bril, his eyes wandering about his sea of books as if he **conned**⑤ the horizon for a sail. "Look yonder, through that window, Monsieur Mignot; tell me what you see in that tree."

"I see a crow," said David, looking.

"There is a bird," said Monsieur Bril, "that shall assist me where I am disposed to shirk a duty. You know that bird, Monsieur Mignot; he is the philosopher of the air. He is happy through submission to his lot. None so merry or full-crawed as he with his **whimsical**⑥ eye and **rollicking**⑦ step. The fields yield him what he desires. He never grieves that his **plumage**⑧ is not gay, like the oriole's. And you have heard,

漂，船让海浪抛来抛去。他只听见海在咆哮。在这片海上航行他既没有海图，也没有指南针。他心想，世界上肯定有一半人在写书。

布里尔先生一直看到诗稿最后一页。他取下眼镜，用手帕揩揩。

"我的老朋友帕皮诺身体好吗？"他问。

"好极了。"戴维答道。

"你有多少只羊，米尼奥先生？"

"昨天数过，三百零九。这群羊走了背运。原来有八百五十，现只剩这个数了。"

"你娶了亲，有个家，日子也过得舒服。羊带给你的好处很多。你赶着羊到野外，呼吸的是新鲜空气，吃的是称心的甜面包。你只要精心看着它们就行，边看边躺在大自然的怀抱里，听树林里山鸟叫。我这些话说得对吗？"

"是这样的。"戴维答道。

"你的诗我全部看过了。"布里尔先生又说道，两只眼望着他的茫茫书海转来转去，好像在寻找一叶孤帆，"米尼奥先生，你往窗外看看，那树上有只什么？"

"我看到一只乌鸦。"戴维一看，说。

布里尔先生道："多亏了这只鸟，要不然我只得多费些口舌。米尼奥先生，你认识那只鸟，它是空中的哲学家。它安心乐命，所以心情舒畅。它眼睛灵活，步子轻快，没有谁比得上它饱食无忧。它的欲望田野都能满足。它从没有因为羽毛不及黄鹂的鲜艳而苦恼。米尼奥先生，上天给它的歌喉你该听见了吧？你认为夜莺比

① contentment
/kən'tentmənt/ n. 满足，知足

② vigilant /'vɪdʒɪlənt/ a. 警戒的，警觉的，警惕的

③ recline /ri'klaɪn/ v. 斜倚，靠，躺

④ verse /vɜːs/ n. 诗，韵文

⑤ con /kɒn/ v. 仔细研究（检查、考虑）

⑥ whimsical /'hwɪmzɪkəl/ a. 想入非非的，异想天开的

⑦ rollicking /'rɒlɪkɪŋ/ a. 嬉耍的，欢闹的；兴高采烈的，快活的

⑧ plumage /'pluːmɪdʒ/ n.（鸟的）全身羽毛

Monsieur Mignot, the notes that nature has given him? Is the nightingale any happier, do you think? "

David rose to his feet. The crow **cawed**[①] harshly from his tree.

"I thank you, Monsieur Bril," he said, slowly. "There was not, then, one nightingale among all those croaks? "

"I could not have missed it," said Monsieur Bril, with a sigh. "I read every word. Live your poetry, man; do not try to write it any more."

"I thank you," said David, again. "And now I will be going back to my sheep."

"If you would dine with me," said the man of books, "and overlook the smart of it, I will give you reasons at length."

"No," said the poet, "I must be back in the fields cawing at my sheep."

Back along the road to Vernoy he **trudged**[②] with his poems under his arm. When he reached his village he turned into the shop of one Zeigler, a Jew out of Armenia, who sold anything that came to his hand.

"Friend," said David, "wolves from the forest harass my sheep on the hills. I must **purchase**[③] firearms to protect them. What have you?"

"A bad day, this, for me, friend Mignot," said Zeigler, spreading his hands, "for I perceive that I must sell you a weapon that will not fetch a tenth of its value. Only last I week I bought from a **peddlar**[④] a wagon full of goods that he procured at a sale by a **commissionaire**[⑤] of the crown. The sale was of the chateau and belongings of a great lord — I know not his title — who has been banished for conspiracy against the king. There are some choice firearms in the lot. This pistol — oh, a weapon fit for a prince! — it shall be only forty francs to you, friend

它快活吗？"

戴维站了起来。乌鸦在树上粗声粗气呱呱叫着。

戴维慢吞吞说道："布里尔先生，我感谢你。只不过，那些东西全是乌鸦叫，就没有一声夜莺唱吗？"

布里尔先生叹口气，说："如果有，我一定会听见。我每个字都看过了。老弟，你的诗就在生活里，别再动笔写吧。"

"谢谢你。"戴维又说，"我这就回家去放羊。"

"要是你肯留下跟我吃中饭，又不怕忠言逆耳，我可以详细向你说说道理。"那位学者道。

诗人回答说："不用了。我这乌鸦就回到田野里，叫唤我的羊去。"

回弗洛伊路上，他胳膊下夹着写的诗，一路上脚步沉重。进镇以后他走到一家店，店主姓齐格勒，是亚美尼亚来的犹太人，凡能到手的货他都卖。

戴维说："朋友，森林里的狼搅得我的羊在山上不得安宁。要不让羊受害我非得买枪不可。你有什么枪呢？"

"这一来今天我得倒霉，米尼奥老兄。"齐格勒把双手一摊说，"看来我卖给你的枪得十成货色一成价钱。上星期我刚从一个游动商贩那儿进了一车货，他是在王上侍卫主持的拍卖场买来的。拍卖的东西是一位大贵族的城堡和财产。我不知道他是什么爵号，只听说他想谋反，被流放了。卖出去的东西里有几把枪是上等货色。这支手

① caw /kɔː/ v. (鸦等)呱呱地叫

② trudge /trʌdʒ/ v. 步履艰难地走, 疲惫(或费力地)走

③ purchase /ˈpɜːtʃəs/ v. 购买; 赢得

④ peddler /ˈpedlə/ n. 小贩
⑤ commissionaire
/kəˌmɪʃəˈneə/ n. 门警, 看门人

Mignot — if I lose ten by the sale. But perhaps an arquebuse —"

"This will do," said David, throwing the money on the counter. "Is it charged? "

"I will charge it," said Zeigler. "And, for ten francs more, add a store of powder and ball."

David laid his pistol under his coat and walked to his cottage. Yvonne was not there. Of late she had taken to **gadding**[1] much among the neighbors. But a fire was glowing in the kitchen stove. David opened the door of it and thrust his poems in upon the coals. As they blazed up they made a singing, harsh sound in the flue.

"The song of the crow! " said the poet.

He went up to his **attic**[2] room and closed the door. So quiet was the village that a score of people heard the **roar**[3] of the great pistol. They flocked thither, and up the stairs where the smoke, issuing, drew their notice.

The men laid the body of the poet upon his bed, awkwardly arranging it to conceal the torn plumage of the poor black crow. The women chattered in a **luxury**[4] of **zealous**[5] pity. Some of them ran to tell Yvonne.

M. Papineau, whose nose had brought him there among the first, picked up the weapon and ran his eye over its silver mountings with a **mingled**[6] air of **connoisseurship**[7] and grief.

"The arms," he explained, aside, to the *cure*, "and crest of Monseigneur, the Marquis de Beaupertuys."

枪——来，你看，够得上给王子用！卖给你只要四十法郎。朋友，这笔买卖我要倒赔十法郎。不过呢，火绳枪……"

"就这一支吧。"戴维说，把钱扔到了柜台上，"有子弹吗？"

"我这就上。"齐格勒说，"再拿十法郎，再给你加好些火药和弹丸。"

戴维把手枪插进上衣里，回到自己住的屋子。伊旺不在家。近来她爱走东家，串西家。但厨房里的炉子还烧着火。戴维打开炉门，把他写的诗塞进了煤炉里。纸烧旺以后炉子唱起歌来，因为装了烟道，声音很粗。

"这是乌鸦叫！"诗人说。

他走到楼上的房间里，然后关上门。镇上很安静，好些人听到了大手枪砰地一响。他们赶到枪响处，见烟从楼上冒出来，都上了楼。

一个男人把诗人的尸体抱到床上，笨手笨脚地摆好，没让这只可怜的黑乌鸦露出破羽毛。女人七嘴八舌说着惋惜话，有两个跑去给伊旺报信。

事事爱管的帕皮诺先生也是首先到场的人。尽管悲痛，他仍不失为行家，捡起枪一看发现了镶的银雕。

"枪上有博贝尔杜依侯爵的纹章和徽号。"他对身旁的牧师说。

---

① gad /gæd/ v. 游荡，闲逛

② attic /'ætɪk/ n. 顶楼，阁楼
③ roar /rɔː/ n. 吼叫，呼啸，轰鸣

④ luxury /'lʌkʃərɪ/ n. 奢侈，奢华
⑤ zealous /'zeləs/ a. 热心的，积极的
⑥ mingle /'mɪŋgl/ v. 使混合，使相混
⑦ connoisseurship /ˌkɒnəˈsɜːʃɪp/ n. 鉴赏家身份